Masaniello of Naples

The Record of a Nine-Days' Revolution

SALZWASSER
VERLAG

Horace Roscoe

Masaniello of Naples

The Record of a Nine-Days' Revolution

Reprint of the original, first published in 1865.

1st Edition 2022 | ISBN: 978-3-75258-902-3

Verlag (Publisher): Salzwasser Verlag GmbH, Zeilweg 44, 60439 Frankfurt, Deutschland
Vertretungsberechtigt (Authorized to represent): E. Roepke, Zeilweg 44, 60439 Frankfurt, Deutschland
Druck (Print): Books on Demand GmbH, In de Tarpen 42, 22848 Norderstedt, Deutschland

MASANIELLO OF NAPLES.

MASANIELLO OF NAPLES.

THE

RECORD OF A NINE-DAYS' REVOLUTION.

BY

MRS HORACE ROSCOE ST JOHN,

AUTHOR OF

"AUDUBON; THE NATURALIST IN THE NEW WORLD,"
"ENGLISHWOMEN AND THE AGE," ETC.

LONDON

1865.

PREFACE.

Although the name of Masaniello is widely known, there exists a general ignorance with respect to the character of that remarkable man. It is chiefly, indeed, through the attractive but untrustworthy medium of Romance that the Neapolitan Patriot has been rendered familiar to the popular mind; since Fiction, Opera, Burlesque, and Ballet have alternately depicted him as a brigand, a stage-hero, or a buffoon.

The conspicuous acts in the life of Masaniello are recorded, it is true, with more or less accuracy by numerous annalists of Naples during the revolutionary period of the year 1647. The majority of these historical writers, however, convey only a vague impression of the real part enacted by Masaniello in the stirring scenes of the time; whilst biographical accounts, professedly more circumstantial, are so falsified by partiality or distorted by prejudice as to render them, with certain exceptions, almost worthless. These records, moreover, are confined to the pages of foreign authors, chiefly Italian, if we omit the translation into English by Howell of the work of Giraffi and the parody of biography by Midon. There is, consequently, a dearth of information on the subject, at least in any form accessible to the general English reader; and my object has been, by diligently investigating every available authority, to represent the character of Masaniello in its true light.

It is a significant fact that the testimony most honourable to Masaniello is found in the narratives of incontestably superior writers; and thus while he is represented as a second Rienzi by Botta and Baldacchini, he is described as a turbulent demagogue, the ringleader of a disgraceful riot, in superficial contributions to Encyclopædias and in the random references of some modern speculators on Italian politics.

Among the authorities which constitute the sources of information respecting the character and career of Masaniello are, the historical works of De Santis, De Turri, Botta, Baldacchini, and the "*Histoire de la Revolution du Royaume de Naples,*" by Mademoiselle de Lussan. In addition there are, the important Diary of Capecelatro; the "Partenope Liberata" of Donzelli, which, as the first account of the Neapolitan insurrection written in the year of its occurrence, is valuable for its rarity and a certain minuteness of detail; the works of Tontoli and Nicolai; those of the Spanish writers Tarsia, Burana, and the Duke de Rivas; while the Reports of the Pontifical and Ducal Agents resident at the Viceregal Court of Naples in 1647, contained in the *Archivio Storico Italiano*, supply interesting and abundant information not only respecting the insurrection, but with regard to the political and social condition of Naples under the dominion of Spain.

INTRODUCTORY

MASANIELLO OF NAPLES.

I.

NAPLES IN THE 17TH CENTURY, ITS RULERS, PRIESTS, AND PEOPLE.

However varied the characteristics which have been imparted to the architecture of Naples according to the different tastes of her successive Norman, German, or Spanish rulers, neither the caprice of kings nor the tyranny of viceroys has possessed power to despoil the queenly Neapolitan capital of the transcendent graces bestowed upon her by Nature.

Fable indeed, with its sometimes philosophic sense, discovered in the ancient and exquisite Parthenope a fitting abode for the Syrens. To them, therefore, tradition has ascribed its origin, rather than to its real founders, the beauty-loving Greeks, who forsook the original enterprise that drew them from the Negropont, when, dazzled by the first view of Parthenope, they resolved to rebuild it under the name of Napoli, or the New City.

No more felicitous site could have offered itself than the spacious plain surrounding the classic city from which a great capital might majestically rise. Sheltering hills bounded its expanse; masses of rock in sharp, bold outline backed these heights, which, gradually softening as they descended into rounded slopes and verdure-clad declivities, drew nearer and nearer to the sea till laved by the peerless waters of that Bay which has been well termed the Bay of Beauty.

Scarcely could their own Hellas, thought the Greeks, surpass in loveliness the radiant expanse of coast and isle-decked sea which Parthenope viewed from its mountain summits yielded to the sight. Its environs too, Pompeii, Baæi, Pozzuoli, rivalled in picturesque charm the famed resorts of Grecian muse or Sibyl. Delphian oracle could ask no more noble shrine than the inspired cave of Cumæ. Waters of Castaly flowed not more purely than did fountain in the delicious shades of Poggio Reale, where poet might find dreamful repose whilst inhaling fragrance of flowers as sweet as rose or violet of Attica could give. Here then the Greek immigrants lingered to found the city which of all the free States of classic Italy was the last to yield its liberty to the grasping Norman aggressor. This was not before Latin and Roman had enriched the soil of Naples with memories of fame. Upon the Pizzofalcone heights Lucullus had dwelt in Sybaritic ease. Upon the shore near the entrance of the Piedegrotta the ashes of Virgil found repose.

Whilst the same exceeding charm in sea and coast and sky lends, after the lapse of ages, unequalled grace to the natural features of Naples, vicissitudes have marked the various edifices of the city, which have undergone alterations in unison with the distinctive tastes and characters of the several dominant races who have occupied the capital. Its architectural glories reached perhaps their proudest development at the period of that dazzling art-regeneration, which, as it flashed over the whole of the Italian peninsula, concentrated in her various cities the many-tinted splendours of the mediæval time.

During the 14th and 15th centuries Naples

was enriched with artistic magnificence. Not in vain did the brilliant court of the Anjou princes attract thither artists and handicraftsmen from all parts of Italy. The city was even then enlarged beyond the narrow circumference it owned under the Normans and Hohenstaufens. It saw cathedrals, castles, palaces, monasteries, and council chambers multiply within its limits. The Castel Capuano indeed was founded as early as the 12th century. The occasional habitation of Suabian and Angevin kings, it became subsequently the seat of the municipal tribunal, and later still the scene of those dungeon horrors which the dethronement of the Bourbons revealed. Its grim records are those of misery and crime. Here a mediæval tragedy was enacted in the terrible assassination of a Caracciolo, grand Seneschal and favourite of Joanna II., who was killed after a banquet by order of Covella Ruffa, Duchess of Sessa—the lady coming out of the ball-room to look in triumph on her victim. Here the Spanish viceroy Toledo established the law courts, and it is in the notorious prisons of the Capuano Castle so many thousands of hapless offenders have languished.

This castle was soon rivalled by the Castel

Nuovo, or New, still so called, though erected six hundred years since by Charles of Anjou, the first French sovereign who reigned in Naples.

To an earlier date belongs the Castel del' Uovo, the work of that Norman King William, well surnamed the Wicked. He it was who converted the rock adjacent to Pizzofalcone cliff into a fortress, and named it *dell' Uovo*, after the shape of the rock, which was that of an egg.

By another Charles of the same lineage as he who erected the Castel Nuovo was built the Church of St Lorenzo, commemorating the celebrated victory over the flaxen-haired Manfred at Benevento, as did the Abbey of Santa Maria the defeat of Conrad at Tagliacozzo. The locality of St Lorenzo, with its venerable church and monastery famed from the remotest times as ground of classic interest, associated with every stirring event in the annals of Naples, and linked as it is with the most important action of the revolt under Masaniello, possesses greater historical attraction than all other points of the city.

In the first half of the 14th century was founded by Robert the Wise the noble edifice originally called St Erasmus, but known to modern times as St Elmo, which, towering in a magnificent situation, commands an unequalled prospect over the city and surrounding territory, and constitutes the chief fortress of Naples. This castle was completed by the Spanish viceroy Toledo in the 16th century, and retains almost entirely to this day the very form it then assumed.

As the boundaries of Naples extended during the middle ages, aristocratic life withdrew from the inner and lower parts of the town, which day by day became more densely peopled. Here was the centre of incessant activity and turmoil, and the nobles and merchant princes of Naples hastened to the higher portions of the western quarter. Hence the abodes of the old nobility within the city were deserted and fell into decay, just as in later times the palaces in the vicinity of Naples have been surrendered to be the bivouac of Garibaldians. Consequently, with the exception of a certain number of important public edifices, less probably remains of the Naples of the middle ages than of other Italian cities. Who indeed would recognize in the Naples of to-day the city as described somewhat more than two centuries ago, when the scene of the revolution under Masaniello?

The influence of the Spanish viceroys, the first of whom assumed office at the commencement of the 16th century, stamped itself materially no less than morally on Naples. At the period of the great insurrection under Masaniello in the year 1647 the city retained in form and extent, as well as in the salient features of its architecture, the characteristics impressed on it a century earlier under the sway of Don Pietro di Toledo, who, although a viceroy of the genuine Spanish stamp, did not abide in Naples without conferring some substantial benefits upon its inhabitants.

A glance at the Naples of the 17th century suffices to show us the contrasts it presented from sea margin to centre, with the city of the present date. Where now the broad sweep of the Riviera di Chiaja extends, with its smooth lava pavement, thronged like the Roman Corso with gay equipages and an eager concourse, representing the toils and needs, the fashion, ease, and luxury of the hour, was at that date a series of villas inhabited by the wealthy. There, amidst foliage and flowers, the lords of Conca, the Sanseverini, the Caraccioli, and other noble Neapolitan families, recreated and enjoyed. Where now, facing the Chiaja, spreads the Villa Reale with its marble temples, fountains and statues glittering amidst long glades of laurel, where green verdure and blue sea shine gloriously in the sunlight of this imperial promenade, was in those days a solitary strand unceasingly washed by the waves. There, as more recently at the Mergellina, fishermen drew their boats to shore, and nobles curvetted their steeds or drove in their gilded chariots along this pictnresque route to the then favourite Church of Santa Maria di Piedegrotta. This strand was first adorned with plantations and flowers by Don Luis de Cerda, Duke of Medina, the last viceroy delegated by the Spanish monarchy to rule in Naples. Of the several structures marking the sea-front of the city, the arsenal, the harbonr, the Royal Palace, the Castel Nuovo—the Bastile of Naples—the Marinella, or southern quay, has perhaps retained most distinctly its original appearance. Its wide beach has served from time immemorial as a rallying point for the Lazzaroni, who are still to be seen here stretched at full length basking in the snn, or standing for honrs idly in the shallow water at the side of their boats.

A greater change than has taken place along the shore has marked the interior of the city since the epoch of the Revolution of 1647. A network of dark, narrow, crooked windings, given up to dirt and gloom and squalor, then intersected the heart of the town. Numerous covered passages, described as dismal caverns by writers* of the time, which now-a-days would furnish inviting quarters to garotters, were then in Naples the resort of thieves and vagrants, who were the terror of honest wayfarers by night and day. Damp hovels, unvisited by the light, were the abodes of destitution and vagabondage, which filled these alleys wherever the space was not occupied by the stalls and shops of petty dealers. Sometimes the whole of the small streets in this crowded neighbourhood were devoted to the followers of a single trade; and were denominated accordingly as the streets of the Orefici, or goldsmiths, the Panettieri, or bakers, the Armieri, or armourers, just as a certain quarter of the town was called La Sellaria from the saddlery business carried on there. As a great majority of the traders in Naples were foreigners—Genoese, Florentines, or French—so the names of streets recalled their several nationalities, such as the Rua Toscana, the Rua Francesca, and the Rua Provenzale. In the midst of this labyrinth of byways, opposite the Strand of the Marinella, stood, supported by its thirty pillars, the Hall of those diligent and unscrupulous traders, the Genoese.

* Giannone, "Storia civile di Napoli," book xxxii. chap. i. Scipione Miccio, "Vita di Don Pietro di Toledo."

It is not surprising that in this quarter, densely peopled, denied free access of light and air, and rendered still more unwholesome by the dank refuse, causing ill odours, of the adjacent market-place, infectious diseases should have constantly broken forth, of which the wretchedly-lodged, ill-fed poor were the chief victims. These visitations of sickness reached their climax in the fearful pestilence which afflicted the city during the year 1656, and which first attacked the miserable quarter of the Vico Rotto al Mercato, the birthplace of Masaniello. As a thanksgiving for its cessation a fresco was added to the Capuan gate, which, like the other gates of Naples, commemorated the termination of similar scourges bred of negligence on the part both of government and people.

The Neapolitans had reason to feel thankful then to a ruler who, like Don Pietro di Toledo, cleared away the numerous nooks and angles which impeded air currents through the streets, and who paved these streets with tiles in addition to draining the insalubrious swamps in the vicinity of Naples. Don Pietro it was, too, who erecting fortresses along the coast from the Papal boundaries to Terracina, kept at bay the pirates of Algiers and Tunis who roved the Adriatic and

Mediterranean seas, and by the erection of these so-called Saracen Towers repulsed the Turks, though the devout Neapolitans could not but ascribe their deliverance to the sole intervention of the Madonna of Carmel. It is just, therefore, that even now the most imposing street of the Neapolitan city should perpetuate the name of the Viceroy, Don Pietro di Toledo. The wretched condition of the humbler classes in the 17th century is easily inferred from the characteristics of the quarter in which they lived.

On the other hand, the wealthy traders and merchant princes vied with the nobility in the splendour of their habitations and luxurious mode of their lives. Whilst those palaces, which are peculiarly the creation of Italy, multiplied in the vicinity of the city, the castles of the feudal aristocracy rose on the lesser heights of the Apennines, and on the Pizzofalcone rock, to which so many of the nobility fled for refuge during the revolutionary storm of 1647. Here, in order to enjoy the exquisite prospect of sea and land the Pizzofalcone affords, a Carafa first took up his abode. His example was followed by numbers of the nobility.

Though a somewhat meretricious style characterized art in Naples during the 17th century, the magnificence of its elaboration is incontestable. Churches and monastic edifices shared in the unparalleled display which distinguished private mansions. Sometimes, as in the church of St Martino, the walls were encrusted with the most exquisitely wrought marblo mosaic. Balustrades of various porphyry, lavishly traced and decorated, were surpassed in magnificence by the sparkling effulgence of the altar, whero agate, jasper, lapis-lazuli, or amethysts were the costly offerings of the earth to the hand of Genius, which set them in a thousand dazzling forms of splendour. The luxury which reigned in the abodes of the wealthy then reached its climax. Within their mansions the renowned Tuscan artists expended the noblest efforts of their skill. Enamellers and gilders exercised their marvellous ingenuity, and beautiful indeed was the furniture of mosaic wrought in woods of various colours inlaid with ivory or more costly substances, representing flowers and landscapes, architecture, or groups of figures. When, in addition, we picture the saloons of the Neapolitans, draped and decorated with the rich gold-inwoven tissues of silk and velvet then in vogue, with the exquisitely cut Venetian glass mirrors, vessels of the precious metals, of Indian porcelain, or carved crystal, with the glittering services of gold and silver in abundant use among the affluent, we are enabled to form some idea of the magnificent mode of living which prevailed among the aristocracy of the time, and to estimate in some measure the stupendous sacrifice of property incurred through the numerous incendiaries which marked the course of the Revolution of 1647.

Such were the contrasts, strange and sad, which marked distinction of class, contrasts more sharply and painfully defined in Naples than in other European capitals. A bitter gulf, widened by selfishness and tyranny, deepened by ignorance and hostility, separated the rich and poor, the Dives and Lazarus of that day, those who occupied the heights of the social scale, and those who, obscure, destitute, and degraded, filled the dark places of the earth. Their cry of anguish at length rose up calling for justice, and the might of the great Nemesis was revealed in the Revolution.

II.

THE RULERS OF NAPLES.

Early in the 11th century the warrior pilgrims of Normandy, visiting southern Italy, repulsed the invading Saracens from its shores. Not altogether disinterested was the succour volunteered by these Christian heroes, for the noble territory they had so promptly rescued from the aggressive infidel in turn became the prey of the champion. Somewhat more than a century later, Naples, the chosen seat of the Greek civilization on Italian soil, submitted to King Roger of the Norman race, already Conqueror and Count of Sicily.

The Neapolitan State, beyond all other territories of Italy, has groaned under the bitterness of foreign rule. It has also endured the additional evil of a perpetual change of masters. The history of Naples shows us how two races above others, the Spanish and the French, have held iron dominion over her; and of these two it would be difficult to say which has wrought the greater amount of misery to the Neapolitans. The vain unscrupulous tyranny of the French sovereigns was perhaps less odious and hurtful than the more systematic but even more repulsive and imperious despotism of Spain.

The brief sway of the Imperial German House of Hohenstaufen, which followed the Norman rule in Naples, was succeeded by that of the Anjou princes, who, with the aid of Papal patronage, founded a monarchy which lasted through the greater part of two centuries till the year 1442. These Angevin rulers introduced the feudal principle, which, blending with the remains of the Greek civilization, produced those special features which in Naples characterized the polity of the state. Hence we find many contrasts as singular as that of the *Sediles*, or *Seggie*, which represented the Athenian *Fratrie*, associated with the fiefdom and vassalage of feudalism.

However famed the magnificence attending the courts of the Anjou princes, their glories grew dim upon the accession of the collateral line of Anjou Durazzo, a race inheriting all the vices without the brilliant qualities of the primary branch. The reign of this lineage consequently was one undeviating succession of crime and revolt.

Seven years after the death, in 1435, of the last queen, Joanna, of this race, Naples became the conquest of the House of Arragon. Two centuries of subjection to Angevin rulers had infused a strong French element into the Neapolitan State. A powerful party, therefore, were speedily in arms against Ferdinand I., the "old fox of Arragon" and friend of Borgia.

The successor of Ferdinand ruled in scarcely less disquietude, and did not cease to tremble for his throne, but even in sleep, harassed by imaginary terrors, was accustomed to cry out "The French are here, the French are here, and the stones and the trees cry out France!" His forebodings were realized when, not long after, Charles VIII. made triumphal entry into Naples at the close of the 15th century.

At this period the true glory of Italy had fled with her independence. The spirit of liberty might have wandered in vain through the length and breadth of the Peninsula to discover an abiding-place. The land of her early welcome was enslaved through the treachery of those who should have been her defenders. Over the rich plains of Lombardy the Viper crest of the Visconti ruled. Florence, the last refuge of independence, was about to lose that independence under the specious sway of the Medici. Every patriotic heart had reason to lament the banished freedom mourned by the Piagnoni. Treason and fraud formed the dominant policy, a policy of which Alexander VI. in Rome and Alphonso of Arragon in Naples were the fitting representatives. In war, venality and debasement resulted from the extinction of all true military spirit, and *Condottieri* in the pay of the Sforza robbers and Papal intriguers usurped the place of those soldier-citizen companies who rallied round the standard of the Commonwealth to preserve to the death the virgin liberties of the early mediæval age. No true war and no solid peace attended the annihilation of freedom in Italy.

The fatal moment of her degeneracy was identical unhappily with the epoch which saw her two most formidable enemies at the summit of their power—France by the recent acquisition of some of the richest territories of her realm, Spain through her final conquest at Granada and the union of Arragon and Castile. The fiercest struggles between the contending powers of France and Spain for rule over the fairest portion of the Italian peninsula involved its inhabitants for centuries in misery and discord. Nor were these afflictions ended when, at the close of the 16th century, Charles V., of renowned memory, receiving the triple crown of the Empire at the hands of Pope Clement VII., became sole possessor of Naples. Then, indeed, was inaugurated an era of unprecedented wretchedness for the Neapolitans under the government of the viceroys of Spain, whose excesses and enormities incurred so dire a chastisement some hundred years later, when a cowardly representative of viceregal authority quailed and fled before the barefooted Apostles of Liberty led on by Masaniello.

Yet the rule of Charles V. was held in grateful remembrance by the people of Naples. His memory was lauded even throughout the course of the Revolution. Its war cry of "Down with the bad government" was united with "Long life to the monarch of Spain," while the great object aimed at was the reacquisition of those rights he had conceded. This apparent contradiction is accounted for by the fact that a wide margin of freedom was enjoyed in all details of government by the viceroys, whose individual character thus powerfully influenced the condition of the people, who reserved to themselves a "right of rebellion in the name of the King," as a safeguard against the encroachments of those delegates from Madrid. When oppressed past all limits of endurance by the misrule of ministers, an embassy was invariably despatched by the Neapolitans to the monarch of Spain, whom they looked upon as the guardian of their liberties. Thus when Charles V., after his campaign in Tunis, was received in Naples by the Viceroy Toledo, the Emperor remarked,—"Don Pietro, I see you are not the violent character I have been told you were." "I see," returned the Viceroy, "I have been described to you as a monster." *

Nevertheless, "almost all the viceroys," writes one of the most accurate of Neapolitan chroniclers,† "through their pride and intolerance were cruel oppressors of the country;" which was indeed regarded as a mine in which the inhabitants were doomed to work as slaves to satisfy the Imperial greed of gold. To meet this end the inhabitants were made to sound the depths of every possible kind of misery.

Don Pietro di Toledo, who assumed office as the first viceroy of Naples in the year 1532, was a man thoroughly Spanish in feeling and devoted

* Scipione Miccio, "Vita di Don Pietro di Toledo."
† Baldacchini, "Storia Napoletana," p. ii.

to the interests of Spain. As the statesman who, beyond all others, gave form and power to that viceregal government which existed in Naples from his accession to office till the time of the Revolution, and whose period of rule was marked by some of the most memorable events in Neapolitan history, his administration calls for special notice.

The type of rule exercised by Don Pietro di Toledo finds a parallel, as it finds supporters, in all ages of history—in the Venetian oligarchy of the middle ages, and in the Imperial principle as it is represented in France at the present day. Material prosperity, at the expense of the life, intellectual and spiritual, was its foundation. Had the physical welfare of the Neapolitans only called for consideration, this ruler might have deserved in some measure the panegyrics lavished upon him by certain writers.* But his system of policy, though fair in appearance, was unsound at the core. Whilst Don Pietro fortified Naples without, he exercised an unbearable despotism within. Whilst he admitted light into the streets, he forbade its entry into the mind. Under pretext

* Miccio, "Vita di Toledo." Giannone, "Storia di Napoli." Filotimo Alicarnasseo, "Vita di Toledo."

of arresting the spread of heresy, he put an end to independent opinion and free discussions; and science and letters were virtually abandoned when certain academies were put under prohibition. He forbade the bribery of judges and the sale of judicial places, but this apparent reform, the reality of which was so greatly needed, owing to the corrupt state of the judicial administration in Naples, was mocked by the barbarity with which Don Pietro caused the ordinances of his so-called reform to be enforced.

The result was that the sacrifices involved in the enactment of the new code were so monstrous as to constitute a fitting holocaust to injustice itself. Not only was the crime of perjury, so prevalent among the Neapolitans, treated with increased severity, but minor offences were visited with such terrible harshness that Don Pietro could boast in a letter to a grand ducal agent in Tuscany, that no less than eighteen thousand persons had died by the hands of the hangman during the eight years of his rule. "He did not know," he confessed, "what more he could do."* Burglaries and night affrays were

* Documenti relativi al governo di Pietro di Toledo. Lettere di Francesco Babbi al Duca di Firenze. Archivio Storico Italiano, vol. ix.

strictly punished, and in such summary fashion that a young noble, having been detected by the police in scaling a prohibited ladder in order to gain the apartment of his inamorata, met the same fate as a common thief, notwithstanding public representations and entreaties in order to save him.

All these enormities the people of Naples might have endured, but not the crowning offence of Toledo in his attempt to introduce the Inquisition. This odious tribunal was actually proclaimed by edict as established, when the entire community, nobles, burghers, and artisans, exasperated into resistance, menacing and defiant, flew to arms. Then it was that another Tommaso Aniello, a name destined to be celebrated in the annals of revolution, constituted himself a leader of the movement. Unlike revolutionary tumults in general, this rebellion owned no distinction of class, for the child-Marquis of Pescara, crucifix in hand, headed the multitude through the streets of Naples. The popular fury was unbounded. In order to quell it, the artillery opened upon the town, and a fierce contest ensued with the Spanish guard and the people in the vicinity of the Castel Nuovo. The summary executions which took place only increased the general hatred of the existing ministry. A council assembled to decide whether to refuse further obedience to Toledo, and whether an embassy should be despatched to Charles V. For the purpose of congregating the citizens, a body of Neapolitans desired to ring the great bell of St Lorenzo, and a certain deputy who tried to prevent them was nearly flung in wrath from the steeple. Banners bearing the Imperial ensign flaunted on the belfry of the venerable seat of the municipal tribunal. Then, as in the second revolution, under another Tommaso Aniello, the Neapolitans were eager to avoid incurring the guilt of rebellion, and then, as in the year 1647, their war-cry was "Long live the Emperor," "Down with the Inquisition." The reply of Charles V. to the embassy despatched from Naples declared he had no intention whatever of introducing the Inquisition, and a free pardon was granted by him to the insurgents, an act of clemency which the rigorous justice of Toledo took care should be but partially carried out.

Under Don Pietro di Toledo it was that development was given to the several departments of administration which constituted the government of Naples under the viceroys of Spain. Perhaps its most remarkable feature was the existence of the *Sediles*, or *Seggi*, or assemblies for the discussion of public affairs generally. The importance of the *sediles* as an element of the Neapolitan constitution can scarcely be exaggerated, since an eminent writer,* who devoted his researches to the study of this particular institution, affirms that "the history of the national life itself is contained in that of the sediles." If these assemblies bore some resemblance to the *fratrie* of the Greeks, the resemblance was still more striking to the Florentine *loggie*, or lodges attached usually to the houses of illustrious families, such as the Cerchi, the Rucellai, and the Buondelmonte, in which they were used to discuss affairs political, public, or private. The Neapolitan sediles, in the same manner, were sometimes called *Piazze*, signifying the squares or places of meeting, and hence the expression "*far piazze*," to assemble the sediles.

It was the custom in Naples, as in many other Italian cities, for members of the same family or lineage to reside together in certain localities. After the families themselves, or after the quarters in which they dwelt, the sediles were usually

* Camillo Tutini, "Dell' origine e fundazione de Seggi di Napoli."

named—the latter generally when in the neighbourhood of a church or gate; as the sediles Capuano and Montagna, Nido, Porta, and Porta Nuova, so denominated in accordance with the several quarters of the city. The first two sediles represented the feudal nobility of the kingdom, the other three the remainder of the nobility; while through the lapse of ages no provision whatever existed for the representation of the popular interests. At the commencement of the 15th century, such was the depressed state of the citizens that they were severely reproved for exhibiting the least evidence of public spirit. When a grocer of Naples requested a noble member of the Porta Nuova sedile to tell him what his Majesty King Charles had decreed with respect to the regulations of the town, he received the insulting reply, "Why do you concern yourself about this city? We are the nobles and citizens of Naples, and you, base outcasts, have nothing to do with it."

The fierce contests for supremacy which arose between the two aristocratic sediles afforded an opportunity to the people for the assertion of their rights, which henceforth received a promise of guardianship in the institution of a sixth sedile, which, somewhat akin to the Florentine *Arti*, represented rather the *popolo grasso*, or superior class of citizens, than the masses.

After the time of Charles of Anjou—the first monarch who took up his residence in the Neapolitan capital—the parliaments, which hitherto had moved with the Court, assembled only in Naples. Increased responsibility and importance were thus conferred upon the sediles, which henceforth indeed superseded the parliaments, as the viceroys usually only summoned the parliaments when unable to carry out their views by means of the sediles. How completely the rights of the people were overlooked through inequalities in a representative system which gave precedence only to aristocratic claims and privileges, is easily seen. Notwithstanding certain concessions to the popular interests made at certain intervals, we find that the injustice of the system continued to be bitterly felt by the Neapolitans, for at the period of the Revolution, under Masaniello, in the middle of the 17th century, their continual demand was that the people should enjoy an equality of votes with the nobility.

As in the case of the noble sediles, there had originally existed in connection with them twenty-nine subordinate sections, which were gradually incorporated into the larger representations, so the popular sedile (*Seggio del Popolo*) included twenty-nine divisions according with certain quarters of the town called *Ottinen*, or eight, owing to the fact that the *Capitani*, or leaders of their several communities, were elected by a body of eight burghers, who were themselves selected in the first instance by the whole of the several communities. The *Capitani* formed a kind of half-military, half-civic police. Sometimes authority over more than one division was entrusted to a single person, as was the case when Masaniello filled the post of *Capitano*.

In the noble sediles the members of certain registered families exercised the right of choosing their *Eletto*, or Deputy. In the popular sedile there existed another form of election. Out of the six persons selected as candidates by the sedile, the viceroys had the right of appointing one. Sometimes they even ordered a new election. Thus it happened that the *Eletti*, or deputies, were, in the majority of cases, mere puppets of the viceroys;* and in the protest against the Inquisition under Masaniello of Sorrento, as well as in the tumult of a later date under Masaniello

* Capecelatro, "Annali della Citta di Napoli," p. ii., part II.

of Naples, the deputies could in no sense be regarded as the exponents of the popular will, but were held in odium, and execrated by the populace.

Under Don Pietro di Toledo was established the *Consiglio Collaterale*, or Upper Privy Council, which constituted the supreme tribunal under the viceregal *régime*. Its members were Neapolitans and Spaniards. Though this council absorbed into itself the most important state offices, the departments of justice, war, and finance, its effect was to strengthen power in the hands of those under the immediate supervision of the Viceroy, who, by removing the seat of the several ministrations of the council to the viceregal palace, established there a ministry entirely subject to his control.

Three courts of justice existed in Naples,—the *Sacro Consiglio*, or Holy Council, whose fifteen councillors decided civil causes; the Court of the Vicariat, consisting of a criminal tribunal and a Court of Appeal for civil suits; and the Supreme Court of Judicature, for judgment of fiscal matters. Notwithstanding the existence under the viceregal government of these various departments for the administration of the laws, the state of justice, in spite of the so-called reforms of Toledo, was wretched in the extreme. Indeed, the very multiplicity of the laws tended to confuse them, and combined with the action of other causes to produce that amount of litigation which afflicted Naples to an unprecedented degree, and "was an evil," writes a Neapolitan Chronicler, "profoundly rooted in our city." A large number of the inhabitants of Naples consequently devoted themselves to legal practice, and bitter complaints are repeated from page to page of the annalists of Naples against the lawyers, who through their nefarious proceedings were too often enriched at the expense of the general community. But justice, like everything else in Naples, had its marketable value; and as law proceedings increased, a richer booty flowed unto the royal treasury.* Occupation for the lawyers was augmented, owing to the number of trials which resulted from a right granted by Charles V., who saw with alarm the increase of feudal power, enabling communities under certain conditions to purchase their freedom from feudal tenures. Many, eager to avail themselves of the privilege, became burthened with debt in order

* Relazione di Napoli del Senatore Girolamo Lippomano.

to buy their release. The sums demanded were sufficiently costly, as we find from the amounts paid by Amalfi and even the little village of Somma. Communities outbid each other until their resources frequently were so involved as to compel them to sell themselves anew in order to cover their liabilities. Villages attached to the Crown were handed over by the viceroy to the highest bidder.

With the sale of territories, titles also were sold, and sometimes even without estates attached. Mock aristocrats, impatient to launch into the lavish display of the time, were speedily ruined. Owing to the continually fresh partition of land and the complicated conditions of its sale and purchase, the relations of property became so involved and so often contested, as to give rise to perpetual legal processes, in which the Neapolitans were the victims of those unscrupulous lawyers against whom historical vengeance so bitterly inveighs. Whether communities were ransomed, or individuals ruined, the one great aim of the government was attained—the exchequer was enriched.

In addition to pecuniary pressure through these sources, there existed in Naples the permanent evil of a burdensome taxation. The financial administration of the viceregal government was indeed a primary source of the calamities that afflicted the State. The fruits of industry were absorbed in satisfying the thirst for gold created by the ceaseless and universal wars of the monarch of Spain. At the time of Toledo's government, the donations or extraordinary supplies, which had hitherto been restricted to their legitimate operation and resorted to only on special occasions, were converted into a system of periodical assessment, and later served as a means of unparalleled and unendurable extortion.

The foundation of the Neapolitan taxation was the personal or family impost known as the *Tassa dei Fuochi*, or hearth tax. The feudatories who paid the *adva*, or feudal tax, were exempt from this. The satisfaction of this impost, therefore, as well as of the donatives, from both of which ecclesiastics were free, fell, together with the payment of the *gabelles*, or indirect taxes, with double weight upon the people, and gave rise to the glaring injustice that those who were the least qualified to do so had the most to pay, and *vice versâ*.*

* Botta, "Storia d'Italia," vol. vi. p. 314. Discorso sulla Storia finanziera del Viceregno. Archivio Storico Italiano, vol. ix.

But the Spaniards regarded the whole machinery of government as nothing more than an expedient to extort money. They wished to reduce the *Sediles*, which had virtually superseded the parliament, into the mere form of a constitution, the object of which was to give an appearance of legality to their proceedings, however unwarrantable. Sometimes the very existence of the *Sediles* was disregarded, as when the Duke of Alva in 1625 suddenly collected an extraordinary tax without the consent of the *Sediles*.

Tho very resources of the revenue were farmed. In a matter of extraordinary taxes, the capital itself was put up for sale, and tho means of realizing its value left to the purchaser. In the case of customs and ordinary taxes, the proceeds themselves were sold. This system of robbery and extortion it was which brought so dire a retribution thereafter on all those who had enriched themselves by speculations in tolls. The traders in these jobberies were chiefly foreigners, and the Genoese* especially were preferred by the Spaniards, on account of the greater securities they offered. Not without reason was it affirmed that "these Genoese devour the king-

* Giannone, "Storia di Napoli." Libro xxxvii. c. 2.

dom, and will only trade to their own great advantage."

In the mean time lawful payments, such as the salaries of magistrates and officials, were stopped. The grossest outrages were committed by the soldiery, who, instead of receiving payment, were allowed, through the connivance of the viceroy, to depredate the kingdom and enrich themselves in that manner. Even the public banks were not allowed to remain unmolested. Every possible artifice was resorted to in order to drain the kingdom of money. Nothing could surpass the brutality exercised by the agents employed in this nefarious extortion. Those who had not a roof to shelter them, a bed to lie on, or a rag to cover them, were still called upon to pay, and told to sell the honour of their wives and daughters if they could raise money in no other way.* By one means or another, money the government would have. Justice, valour, intellect, were appreciated only in proportion to their marketable value. Everything was put up to auction. The State resembled one vast market, in which everything was bought and sold to satisfy the craving of the Spanish horse-

* Botta, "Storia d'Italia," vol. vi. p. 316.

leech, which still was insatiable. "The kingdom is reduced to the direst extremities," writes a representative of one of the Italian States, "we are in an abyss." *

In spite of this national misery, the viceroys contrived to live at ease amidst luxury and indulgence of every kind. A current saying was that no one should wish to occupy the post of viceroy at Naples, to avoid all chance of the possible pain of having to relinquish it. The incomes received by the viceroys were considerable; but their receipts, from the sale of offices and from the various mediums through which bribery and corruption operated under Spanish rule, added to the donations which under different pretexts they contrived to amass at the expense of the citizens, probably reached a sum which equalled, if it did not exceed, the amount of the viceregal salary itself.

Don Pedro Giron, Duke of Ossuna, who assumed office in the year 1616, represented *in excelsis* the reckless extravagance in which the Spanish viceroys were accustomed to indulge.

* Documenti degli agenti in Napoli del Duca d'Urbino, e del Gran Duca di Toscana. Archivio Storico Italiano, vol. ix.

Under his rule it was that the "*spese segrete*" (private expenditure), which had previously figured in the pecuniary programme of viceroys at the cost of forty thousand ducats annually, increased from 1616 to 1619 to the egregious amount of three hundred and eighty thousand ducats.* Such was the pomp in which the Duke of Ossuna lived, that it was remarked by a nobleman who paid him a visit once, that "he thought he was going to pay a visit to the viceroy of Naples, but he had been received by the king of Spain."

The Duke's carriage, adorned with gold embroidery within, was adorned with jewels without. The silver upon it alone was estimated at two hundred pounds. "It is a chariot worthy of a king," writes the Tuscan agent. When flaunting in it through the city, the Duke was accustomed to scatter gold and silver coins through the windows amongst the people, a favourite device with viceroys, who desired to court popularity, but resorted to in vain by the Duke of Arcos when the revolutionary storm of 1647 darkened over Naples. The viceroys could well afford to squan-

* Lodovico Bianchini, "Della Storia delle finanze del Regno di Napoli."

der small coin in return for the donations they received. It was as though they took the people's meals and made a gracious merit of giving them the crumbs.

The viceregal establishments were characterized by the ceremonial and magnificence of a royal residence; where, in addition to trains of domestics, congregated a motley throng of dignitaries, civil, ecclesiastical, and military. The viceroys entered the city with all the pomp of sovereigns and with all the pride of conquerors.* It was their custom to remain in the environs of Naples at one of the palaces of the nobility till their predecessors had fairly departed. One of those richly-decorated feluccas, with coloured sails, gilt carving, and vivid paintings, so much in use among the nobles of the time, then conveyed the viceroy to the harbour, where the quay was draped with crimson damask, and canopied for the occasion. The inauguration of the viceroy in office was celebrated with deafening volleys of artillery.

If magnificence attended the entry of the viceroys into the city, they were determined that profit should attend their departure. Large sums, which had been extorted under pretence

* Vita di Pietro Toledo da Scipione Miccio

of the Emperor's requirements, were appropriated to their own use.* It was not enough for these viceregal robbers to plunder the country whilst in office, but the miserable infatuation of the people yielded them large donations on their retirement. The Duke of Alva received at his departure seventy-five thousand ducats, without a word of thanks, according to aristocratic custom. During the six years' administration of the Count of Monterey, not above seventeen millions of the forty-three millions of ducats which had been extorted from the people went into the royal coffers. The remainder was appropriated. No less than forty-three vessels were required to carry away this viceroy's possessions at his departure. Sculpture and other works of art were among the accumulation of treasures.†

The public processions of the viceroys on festive occasions were attended with the greatest splendour, and a degree of etiquette which only Spaniards could have tolerated. The Duke of Alcalà, when performing a pilgrimage of de-

* Capecelatro, "Annali della Citta di Napoli," p. 31. Botta, "Storia d'Italia," p. 315.

† Capecelatro, "Annali di Napoli," p. 95.

votion to a certain chapel in Amalfi, took four days in reaching his destination, since he, with his numerous suite, tarried each day to be regaled by noble and archbishop, who kept high holiday.

The old expedient of despotism was effectually employed by the viceroys. With perpetual festivals, tournaments, and banquetings, they pandered to a frivolous love of pleasure too common among the Neapolitans. The result was a degeneracy through which all public spirit was lost, and all patriotic influence undermined. Nobles, who were descended from those of proud name, who had earned renown in the train of many a bold conqueror, were openly insulted by the arrogant Spaniards. The Duke of Alcalà summoned a large company of the most illustrious among the aristocracy to his palace at Posilippo; and after having made them wait his pleasure for hours in the ante-rooms, sent a message to inform them that their attendance was not required by his Excellency, since he had changed his mind. The Duke of Monterey and the Duke of Medina, when viceroy, openly scoffed at the rights of the *sediles*, and by a simple edict tried to impose an increased tax upon wheat.

Extravagant luxury was exhibited in a thousand senseless caprices. The imperious Duke of Ossuna on one occasion invited to an entertainment more than a hundred illustrious ladies of blood so pure that they could not be waited upon except by their own relations. The Duke himself, too transcendently superior to sit at table, even with this distinguished company, looked on through a window out of his special retreat till the repast was concluded, when he emerged in gorgeous attire, and the remnants of the banquet were thrown by the dainty fingers of the lady attendants into the court of the arsenal.* At a ball given by his Vice-duchess every article of the costly attire, even to the shoes worn by the ladies, was furnished at the expense of the viceroy. Not always would the Vice-duchess permit such gracious benevolence on the part of her lord, but on one occasion whipped a lady of the court severely with her slipper because her husband had been installed in office by the Duke.

Notwithstanding the assumption of punctilio on the part of rulers, and an incessant clamour concerning etiquette amongst the nobles, which frequently led to violent feuds, such was the

* Francesco Zazzera, "Del Governo di duca d'Ossuna."

encouragement given to the *donne di libera vita* that the annals of the time are filled with decrees and prohibitions concerning them. When it was suggested that the infamous quarters of Naples should be shut up, the answer was that half the city would be closed. What the laws denounced society sanctioned. By the Duke of Ossuna, at one of those feasts to the people which the viceroys were accustomed to give in the environs of Naples, a table was expressly prepared for twenty-five of the most notorious courtesans. Women of illustrious family, such as the Princess Conca and the Marchesa Campolattro, were not ashamed to be the acknowledged mistresses of the viceroys.

Licence in morals and coarseness in manners render the social history of the period one continuous chronicle of scandals, riots, and the most unblushing depravity. Even during the sacred festivals of the church, intrigues were shamelessly carried on, or affrays arose owing to some trifling offence to the mock majesty which it was the fashion of the day for people to assume. In the midst of religious processions, quarrels would occur as to precedence in the order of march according to rank. A learned doctor, when making a speech at an assembly, forgot to give the title of *Eccelentissimo* to the Prince del Colle, who seized a sword to chastise the offending speaker, but hit by mistake an old man on the head, who was severely wounded.

The lawlessness and violence of the nobles exceeded all bounds. No one who unluckily found himself in the ill-lighted streets of Naples at a late hour was safe from aggression Nocturnal brawls, which often had their origin in the excitement of the gaming-table, were of constant occurrence; and as swords or daggers were usually worn by the Neapolitan cavaliers, life was frequently sacrificed in these senseless struggles.

The passion for duelling was as great as that for gambling. Under the Duke of Medina's government five duels were fought in seven days by different noblemen. The decrees of Toledo were as ineffectual to repress the evil in Naples as were the efforts of Cardinal Richelieu in France. These sanguinary conflicts had their source in the most ridiculous trifles, from a boundary limit to a lap-dog.

Bands of bravoes were retained on the estates of the feudal lords, and employed, as by Don Diomed Carafa during the revolution of the year 1647, for the most iniquitous purposes. These desperadoes, when their masters were too cowardly to enter into conflict themselves, or desired to escape detection in crime, acted as their proxies.

A noble was enamoured of a young girl in humble life who resolutely rejected his infamous suit. Forthwith the traitor commissioned a Spanish hireling to wreak his vengeance on its innocent object, and the young girl was mortally shot whilst standing at a window.*

The Duke of Noya caused a domestic to be seized for some insignificant matter, and sent him back to his master with his nose and ears cut off. The laws of Heaven and man were set at defiance. Nobles and viceroys emulated each other in ferocious licence. The use of the torture was of very frequent occurrence. "Tomorrow," reports the Tuscan agent, "justice is to be done, and many will be put to the rack."

Under the viceroyalty of the egotistic and tyrannical Duke of Ossuna, the most hideous punishments followed accusation without judicial process intervening at all. One person was scourged, another hanged, and another put to the torture in quick succession. What wonder then that bonfires were kindled and joy bells rung at the

* Capecelatro, "Annali di Napoli."

departure of this Caligula of the mediæval age?

These atrocious excesses of despotism reached their climax in the 17th century. The rulers of the unhappy Neapolitans had for ages done their utmost to impoverish, demoralize, and degrade their subjects. It is not strange that revolt and hatred should have been engendered in their hearts. Dark, unseen, but ripening into terrific force, sedition was silently brooding within the limits of that hapless State. But its rulers perceived not the abyss which menaced them. Holding the places of this world's power, they still kept high revelry, and recklessly footed their fantastic death-dance upon the edge of ruin, as though its depths existed not. Court gaieties, rivalling the levities of the Trianon if not the profligacies of the Parc aux Cerfs, were in Naples, as later in France, the masquerading heralds which announced Revolution.

It fell to the lot of Don Roderigo Ponce de Leone, Duke of Arcos, to enter upon office as viceroy at this disastrous crisis. The resources of the kingdom were at the lowest ebb. The arrears of the last donative could not be met. Without, the French were menacing, and their squadron had even entered the gulf; within, there was another foe as yet unheeded, but more portentous still. Inefficient troops and unprovisioned fortresses only were at the command of the Duke of Arcos. To clear the standing debt, the Duke had recourse to the tax on fruit, and the deadly mine of sedition was fired. The Duke of Arcos assumed office in 1646. The elements warned him from the shores which were to prove fatal to his peace. So violent a storm raged as he approached the harbour* that the vessel could with difficulty enter. The lapse of another year saw the man who had come to rule with rigour a craven fugitive from a people infuriated by oppression.

* Baldacchini, "Storia Napoletana," p. 7.

III.

THE PRIESTS OF NAPLES.

"Monks and their riches," writes Giannone, whenever alluding to the monastic orders in Naples; "since," he adds, "monasticism and avarice are inseparably connected."

It might indeed be said the inhabitants of Naples were tyrannized over by two governments—the viceregal and the priestly, both of which were equally oppressive and demoralizing. The arbitrary nature of the Roman ecclesiastical jurisdiction was chief among the sore evils which afflicted the Neapolitan State. The imperious legates of the Pope, not content with the boundless influence exercised by them in their spiritual capacity over the minds of the devout and credulous Neapolitans, assumed a domination in temporal matters which desired to own no limits.

To maintain the just claims of the Papal supervision, to guard the rights of the Apostolic Chamber, and to gather in its rich emoluments, the legitimate aim of their office did not satisfy an ambition which sought its end in the most preposterous encroachments of monopoly. A road could not be constructed from Naples direct into Puglia without the ecclesiastical sanction,* and consent was withheld because the traffic which had hitherto passed through Benevento would in this way be directed elsewhere, to the detriment of the Apostolic Chamber and its dues. In some cases these egregious assumptions of Papal power led to unparalleled slavery. The payment of a small sum to a person who wished to work an alum mine sufficed to keep the mine in Papal bondage, nor was it allowed to be excavated in order that the same product might be sold to greater advantage in the Roman Ecclesiastical State. In consequence of these aggressions, bitter contests rose between the ministers monarchical and the ministers pontifical, which usually ended in mandates, censures, assaults, excommunications, and open warfare. Another source of discord and distress was thus opened, and necessarily did not exist without causing greater misery to the Neapolitan people.

* Corrispondeuza tra il Nunzio di Napoli e la Corte di Roma. Di Roma, Sept., 1599; Archivio Storico Italiano, vol. ix.

The rapid increase of monastic orders in Naples during the 16th and 17th centuries corresponded with the progress of those calamities which undermined the State in its universal relations, political and social.

As the kingdom continued to be drained of reproductive capital, the pursuit of many useful and ingenious arts was to a great extent relinquished. Public offices, in which fraud and tumult reigned, were often willingly abandoned, and those who abandoned them sought the quietude of the cloisters. Thus voluntarily a considerable proportion of the population became a burthen on the trammelled and unrewarded industry of the rest.

It is the impulse of human nature to seek religion rather as a refuge and solace in times of suffering than as a means of elevating and purifying the soul when in the full enjoyment of freedom from depressing influences. Thus, the more wretched and impoverished the Neapolitans were, the more zealously did they sacrifice themselves in order to protect and cherish those to whom they looked for spiritual guidance and control, the more did they, with blind infatuation, contribute to the wealth of those who were already enriched at their expense. What though the original laws of priestly communities enjoined the strictest poverty? Under the specious title of *offerings*, the acceptation of incalculable wealth was rendered lawful, even without those convenient dispensations, exemptions, and privileges, which the Pope was ever ready to sell. The easy-natured Neapolitans readily yielded to the most exorbitant demands of priests or rulers. Lavish endowments were eagerly volunteered. The exemption of ecclesiastics from the imposts under which they themselves were ground down was not enough. It did not satisfy their desire to deal generously by their spiritual advisers. When the sect of the Theatines, who rivalled the Jesuits in power and opulence, came into Naples from Venice, they were received with marked distinction. But the offer of two princely mansions for their accommodation was despised. The Theatines threatened to leave the city in case they were not more suitably housed, when Don Pietro di Toledo, to prevent such a calamity, presented them with the entire parish of St Paul.* A number of superb monastic edifices were speedily erected by this order, notwithstanding their professed tenets of poverty, and a guilelessness

* Giannone, "Storia di Napoli," Lib. xxxii. p. 192.

which rivalled the unconscious trust of the lilies of the field! The most vigilant of all the servitors of Rome were the Theatines, who, as rigorously as Don Pietro himself, guarded against the entrance of German heresy into Naples. The Neapolitans, in gratitude for such watchfulness, not only endowed them with lavish offerings, but erected a statue in bronze to their founder, and affixed his likeness to the gates of the city.

The Jesuits did not profit less by the generosity of the Neapolitans. Their magnificent colleges were so extensive that a single one covered the space of more than one entire street, and the number gradually amounted to not less than two hundred and ninety-three.

These powerful and opulent sects flourished in the midst of a multiplicity of others, none of which were without rich endowments and noble edifices dedicated to their use. Dominicans, Carthusians, Augustines, Benedictines, Carmelites, Capuchins, Franciscans, disciples of Philip Neri, St Joseph, and Saint Theresa, swarmed within the city. Monastic sects, indeed, multiplied to such an extent that a fresh enumeration was required every twenty or thirty years to include their increasing numbers.

So powerful was the sway exercised by the

monks over the people, that to enrich the priesthood was considered by the Neapolitans a duty paramount to all others, and donations and legacies wero accorded them by their disciples, regardlessly of every other consideration, even the rightful claims of kindred or friends. Gold, silver, and precious stones were poured into the priestly coffers incessantly. The simplest relics were the sources of enormous profit. A single miraculous image of the Virgin, said to have been found by the Dominicans, when exhibited, brought in a sum which sufficed for the erection of one of the most magnificent monasteries in Naples.*

Not always through sources so pure as the simplicity of the Neapolitans were the monks enriched, since it was a maxim of the priests that all whose consciences were burthened with the possession of ill-gotten gains should receive pardon and peace on delivering their booty to the Church. The Benedictines of Monte Vergine even shared in the spoils of the criminals whom, through the right of asylum granted to churches and monasteries, they defended. Two-thirds of the State revenues were estimated to be swallowed

* Giannone, "Storia di Napoli," Lib. xxxiv. p. 405.

up by ecclesiastics. It was the remark, indeed, of foreigners who visited Naples, when witnessing the prosperity of the monastic orders, that if a check were not put upon their avarice they would speedily engross the entire city, and in the space of a century become the masters of the whole kingdom.

But a still worse evil than the preponderance of the ecclesiastical orders themselves was the existence of a villanous class who adopted the robes of the Church as a cloak for their great crimes and in order to escape their punishment at the civil tribunal.* These sham priests were generally hirelings of the feudal lords, and, like their masters, were accustomed to indulge in ferocity and licence of every conceivable description. Their costume was the *Mezza Sottana*, or *Tabano*, and they passed under the name of *Tabanelle*, owing to the peculiar fashion of their garments, which were well calculated to conceal whatever weapons they chose to carry. Hence the clause of the edict promulgated under the rule of Masaniello prohibiting this apparel.

* Baldacchini, "Storia Napoletana," p. 28. Corrispondenza tra il Nunzio di Napoli e la Corte di Roma. Archivio Storico Italiano, vol. ix.

Although severe enactments existed against the adoption of this attire, the wearers of it generally contrived, through the influence of their lordly protectors, to escape detection, or at all events punishment.

The most grievous abuse arose from the right of asylum in churches and monasteries, which was increased by the large number of those edifices in Naples. The most heinous crimes were committed with impunity by those who fled to these sanctuaries, until at length the sacred altar became the rallying point of bandits and miscreants, and ecclesiastical edifices the receptacles of vagabondage.* It is true that a secular officer possessed a power of search over these asylums, yet the consequence of this was not to meet the ends of justice, but to engender perpetual altercations as to right of jurisdiction between the civil and ecclesiastical authorities. Terrible affrays consequently often arose in the vicinity of the churches, which were thus made the scenes of sacrilegious scandals. Divine service frequently could not proceed owing to the tumult and riot without. Even the Papal Nuncio,

* Corrispondenza tra il Nunzio di Napoli e la Corte di Roma. Archivio Storico Italiano, vol. ix.

in his correspondence with the Court of Rome, affirmed that so lax had the discipline of the monks become that there was no atrocity they would blush to commit. Letters from the legate record how bandits and malefactors were encouraged by the ready refuge afforded them in the monasteries, and how consequently their profligate audacity increased; while the conduct of the priestly orders is commented upon as notoriously injurious to the Church.

The Pope in return for the information granted full powers to the Nuncio for the suppression of such disorders, and a letter from Rome* invests him with authority to command the superiors of conventa to desist from sheltering offenders. But the inefficiency of Papal proclamations is proved by their repetition. Envoys of Rome and viceroys of Spain alike did little for which the Neapolitans had reason to thank them.

* Lettere di Roma. Archivio Storico Italiano

IV.

THE PEOPLE OF NAPLES.

MEANWHILE what was the condition of the people—those unheeded hundreds whom Strength, born of Labour and Necessity, renders invincible to uphold or destroy a State? Under the influence of a demoralizing government they were daily becoming more and more a source through which its power was undermined and its very existence menaced. When we consider the enormities perpetrated at Naples in the name of authority, this is intelligible without giving acquiescence to the calumniating assertions of a certain annalist of the 17th century, who characterizes the lower orders of Naples as "inclined to tumult and rebellion, and accustomed to trample under foot all legal and moral laws." Rather might the much-enduring Neapolitans have been likened to those

Athenians to whom it was said by Demosthenes, "Shall you always resemble those athletes who, struck in one place, cover it with their hand,—struck in another place, they put their hand there, and thus always occupied with the blows they receive, do not know either how to strike or to defend themselves?"

Naples, rich in natural products, was richer still as the centre of an active trade. Some of the most superb fabrics which luxury could command issued from her factories, while many of those artistic inventions peculiar to the genius of Italy were successfully developed by her artisans. Yet the Neapolitan people derived no benefit either from the surpassing fertility of their native soil, which crowned the least arduous essays of agriculture with countless golden harvests, or from the more ingenious toils of their handicraft. Throughout the length and breadth of the land, from the resplendent orchards of Pozzuoli to the pastures of the Abruzzi, a depressing taxation and monopoly prevailed. In the provinces and the city the paralysing influence was felt. The rough peasant of the Basilicata, and the simple, poor, hard-working inhabitants of the Principata, alike suffered, until anguish gave birth to hatred, and out of endurance arose defiance. If in the

Calabrian borders, invariably rife with sedition, the intractable mountaineers, so far from rendering obedience to oppressive rule, indulged in open lawlessness, the squalid, wrangling population of the Terra di Lavoro, and the forlorn inhabitants of the Mercato were, in secret, not less seditiously disposed. Restless and eager for strife, they hastened to take up arms and join the revolutionary *mêlée* of the year 1647.

An element still more inimical to the State than even these desperate classes was the existence of that singular complex type of the vagrant order, a combination of gipsy, thief, and beggar in one, known, as peculiar to Naples, under the name of Lazzaroni. There are various opinions as to the origin of the denomination. The most simple and probable assumption is, that it was derived from the Christian disciple Lazarus, whose piety has for ever sanctified the cause of poverty, and whose name has descended to its most forlorn inheritors. One of the most accurate of Neapolitan chroniclers refers, however, to a curious suggestion which is to be met with in the manuscript writings of Capecelatro with reference to the origin of the Lazzaroni. According to this statement the denomination was derived from the name of the man who founded an abode of industry in the square of the market-place at Naples, where the poorest of the Neapolitans were accustomed to follow their arduous occupation of preparing leather, a calling which in all probability gave the title of Conciaria to this quarter of the city.

Had the Neapolitans been permitted to reap the just reward of their own industry, wealth would not have been exclusively in the hands of aristocrats and ecclesiastics. Trades of various kinds were busily followed in the city, as the names of the several streets and quarters inform us. Venetians, Genoese, and Florentines had not in vain brought the exercise of their matchless ingenuity into Naples. Every nook and angle in the heart of the town was the scene of stirring toil. Luxurious merchandise, such as rich velvets, and those gold inwoven fabrics originated by the Venetians, constituted, in addition to their own cloths of surpassing excellence, and the fine wool yielded by the flocks which fed on the Abruzzi, the staple products of Neapolitan manufacture. But more important than all as a branch of trade was the production of that unrivalled silk which to this day shares with Genoese velvet a proverbial repute. A large majority of the inhabitants of the city and its environs were supported solely by this manufacture, for the factories of Calabria and Amalfi yielded the splendid tissue in abundance.

In one sense, indeed, Naples was justly reputed to be one of the richest cities of Europe. Whatever in the shape of luxury the varying skill of the several States of Italy had produced, was concentrated within its limits, where from hearth to altar the taste of the time was shown in costly and lavish display. Foreign artists and merchants settled in the city, and the influx thus acquired again gave an impetus to industry.

But there existed in Naples a mischievous class, who covered their avarice under the guise of commercial enterprise, who might more appropriately have termed themselves usurers than traders. Notwithstanding the riches of Naples, money was a costly article to purchase. The demand for it, nevertheless, was incessant, and the supply was afforded by those, chiefly foreigners, who, having large sums to lend, could invariably find borrowers at exorbitant interest. Fortunes were thus rapidly acquired, and with them titles and territories. Hence we find the names of certain families enriched through these sources, transmitted as illustrious—such as the Spinola, Serra, and Ravaschieri,—more than one of whom became unfortunately conspicuous during the Revolution under Masaniello.

The mass of the people meanwhile were the victims of this ruinous system of usury and robbery. They toiled, it is true, but not for their own benefit, just as they fought, though neither for the protection of their liberties nor the defence of their native land. The ceaseless wars of the Emperor Charles required constant supplies of men no less than money, and were thus the source of a twofold evil to Naples. In Lombardy, in Spain, in the Low Countries, and in Germany, the Neapolitans were fighting while their own shores remained unprotected, except by the foreign soldiery who filled the garrisons of Naples. The military establishment was maintained at a great expense, yet the several departments were so infamously mismanaged that the condition of the troops was miserable in the extreme.

The caprice of the viceroys heightened the evil. Command of the troops was often entrusted to incapable or unscrupulous leaders, in order to indulge the favouritism shown by rulers. The Count of Monterey, when viceroy, did not hesitate to deprive veteran and trustworthy Neapolitan captains of the commands they held, in order that their posts might be filled by his own favourites.*

A trustworthy witness describes the pitiful condition of the troops as "shoeless and scantily clad, they having sold everything to appease their hunger."

The Spanish soldiers frequently arrived in Naples so destitute as to earn the title, given them in mockery, of the *Bisogni*, or The Needy.† Owing to the absence of food and pay, they were accustomed, as we have said, to rob publicly. So degenerate had the whole system of warfare become, even since the introduction of mercenaries and the employment of *Condottieri*, that whole regiments resembled little else than bands of robbers, who, though often commissioned to extirpate bandits, were in reality as lawless themselves.

But in every case it was the people who, oppressed and plundered, whether by the quartering of troops, the extortion of tax collectors, or the tyrannous restrictions of rulers, were the first to suffer. To such misery was the State reduced that many families in the pro-

* Capecelatro, "Annali della Citta di Napoli."

† Documenti degli agenti del Duca d'Urbino. Zazzera, "Governo del Duca d'Ossuna."

vinces voluntarily abandoned their native land. They were not able to exist under the exactions of its rulers.* The Duke of Medina, indeed, when viceroy, boasted that he had left the kingdom in such straits that scarcely half a dozen families could make a good meal.† Some parts of the country became utterly deserted, and fertile fields, which should have yielded abundance, were neglected. So abject was the distress the Neapolitans were reduced to through these combined causes, that when Cardinal Zapata, a viceroy who assumed office at the beginning of the 17th century, entered Naples, he was met with lamentations by the people, who were wailing and crying for bread. When, on the visit of the Pope's ambassador, the Cardinal Zapata accompanied him in public, the people cried "Food, food," and threw a piece of bread, which had, says the historian, more of earth than flour in it, into the carriage. The conscientious viceroy, who had come to rule on the same principle as his predecessors in despotism, found occasion thereon to smile.

* Botta, "Storia d'Italia," vol. vi. p. 314.

† Baldacchini, "Storia Napoletana," p. 6.

"Your Excellency should not smile," was the rebuke of the venerable ambassador, "for truly there is cause for weeping."

CHAPTER I.

MASANIELLO OF NAPLES.

Tommaso Aniello, or, as he is best known, through a popular abbreviation, Masaniello, though commonly called of Amalfi, was by nature, by birth, and by parentage, a genuine Neapolitan. His father, Francesco Aniello, a Neapolitan, was united in marriage to Antonia Garegano, who was also a Neapolitan, on the 18th of February, in the year 1620.* In the same year their son, Tommaso Aniello, more familiarly known as Masaniello, was born in the Vico Rotto al Mercato—the most wretched quarter in the city of Naples, the poorest, the dirtiest, and the most densely populated. At the same place another son was subsequently born to Antonia and Francesco, and some years

* Discorso del Luigi Volpicella della patria e della famiglia di Tommaso Aniello—stampata nel, vol. iii. Degli atti dell' Accademia Consentina.

later a daughter, whom they named Grazia Francesca.

Tradition, which is accustomed to shed a halo of romance around the infancy of the illustrious, records how a Capuchin friar, visiting Masaniello while yet in his cradle, foretold to him a lofty destiny. Obscurity, however, veils the outset of his career. What was the early training of Masaniello? What were the characteristics, pursuits, and pleasures of his childhood? We know how restricted were the means of enlightenment existing for the poorer classes of Naples. Did some veritable member of a monastic order interested in his infancy become the instructor of his early years? The inferences to be drawn from the events of his later life alone answer these inquiries, and we are led to conclude that his mental capacities were of a high order, since they were not inadequate to meet the responsibilities of his position as ruler over a noble city.* The admirable measures adopted by Masaniello when administrator, in civil and mili-

* Baldacchini, "Storia Napoletana," pp. 104, 105. Documenti deglia genti del Gran Duca di Toscana in Napoli. Archivio Storico Italiano, vol. ix. Lettere del Cardinal Filomarino. Botta, "Storia d'Italia," vol. vi. Gabriele Tontoli, "Il Masaniello," p. 48.

tary affairs, testify to his having possessed knowledge, both accurate and ample, on subjects of primary importance.*

Though idleness and moral laxity, in the lowest forms of theft and beggary, too often disgraced the lower orders of Naples in common with the Lazzaroni, the exemplary industry which chroniclers unite in attributing to Masaniello, together with his acknowledged nobility of spirit,† form a warrantable ground of presumption that he was free from the vices incidental to his class.

In April of the year 1641, Tommaso Aniello was married to Beradina Pisa, a young and pretty Neapolitan.‡

The portrait of Masaniello, transmitted by history, represents this remarkable man as no ill-favoured suitor for a maiden's hand. He was of the middle height, well formed, and slender.

* Botta, "Storia d'Italia," vol. vi. p. 326. Documenti del carteggio degli agenti del Gran Duca di Toscana. Tontoli, "Il Masaniello," p. 48.

† Botta, "Storia d'Italia," vol. vi. p. 318. Tontoli, "Il Masaniello," p. 93. Lettere del Cardinal Filomarino, Archivio Storico Italiano, vol. ix.

‡ Discorso del Luigi Volpicella degli atti dell' Accademia Consentina. Diario di Francesco Capecelatro.

His complexion was sunburnt, and his fine dark eyes contrasted effectively with his long fair hair, which hung in curls about his neck. His grave and even melancholy countenance was singularly at variance with his vivacity* of manner in action or discourse. When silent, absorbed in reflection, he was habitually pensive. In speaking he was quick and animated, and gave evidence of that restless, impulsive temperament which, nervous and highly-wrought, inclined him to extremes in all things.†

Masaniello wore the fisherman's ordinary garb of white and blue linen, leaving the leg bare below the knee, and the Neapolitan mariner's cap.‡ Yet this simple dress, owing to the peculiarity of its arrangement and its blended colours, was stamped with the identity of the wearer, and appeared at once striking and picturesque. A certain grace of bearing and beauty of aspect lent a charm to Masaniello's whole demeanour, such as that ascribed by Petrarch to Rienzi.§ No wonder, then, that with attributes

* Giraffi, "Rivolutioni di Napoli," p. 11.

† Baldacchini, "Storia Napoletana," p. 24.

‡ Giraffi, "Rivolutioni di Napoli," p. 11.

§ Botta describes Masaniello as possessing "*un certa*

so attractive—a lively fancy, a charming manner and sprightliness in discourse, Masaniello was truly beloved by the people of Naples, who were devoted to him.

Masaniello's employment as a fisherman* consisted in a small commerce carried on with the Neapolitan market. He inhabited a miserable cottage on the market-place at Naples. The spot is remarkable as having been the scene of numerous tragedies. There executions took place, and a scaffold was erected opposite a narrow street, named del Sospirò, as it was from thence the criminal or victim first caught sight of the place of suffering.

The domiciles inhabited by the poor, to whom the quarter where Masaniello lived was allotted, were little better than cells. These gloomy tenements, some of them centuries old, were unvisited by a ray of sunshine, and crowded the dark, damp alleys and narrow windings, which formed a perfect labyrinth of dirt and destitution in the heart of the city during the 17th century. These dim but busy regions, resounding with the

venustà e grazia chi da tutta la sua persona spirava." Storia d'Italia, vol. vi. p. 318.

* "Diario" di Capecelatro, p. 14.

hum of incessant toil, were justly feared as the Faubourg St Antoine of Naples. This portion of the town, densely peopled, as we have said, was also the least airy, owing to the narrowness of the streets, and this was a prolific source of untimely death or lingering disease. Here dwelt numbers of those who first took part in the rebellion under Masaniello. Yet such was the miserable condition of the Lazzaroni that, oftener than not, they could not command even the shelter afforded by such wretched receptacles of mingled want and misery, and often crime, as the dwellings in and about the market-place. The Lazzaroni — ill-omened outcasts — were accustomed to brave all seasons. After a day of wandering or toil on the scantiest subsistence, they would look to the shadow of a portico for refuge, or find shelter under the huge baskets that constituted their chief possession.

The dwelling of Masaniello on the market-place was distinguished from the rest only through having the name and arms of the Emperor Charles V. engraven on the balcony.* This circumstance Masaniello is said to have frequently commented on, ascribing it to a

* Giraffi, "Rivolutioni di Napoli," p. 12.

mysterious presage that *he* should restore those privileges which the Emperor Charles had granted to the city.*

Masaniello possessed the true Neapolitan attributes of enthusiasm and eloquence, which were united in him to a spirit of boldness which knew no fear.† He possessed a lofty and generous soul; ‡ and throughout the course of his chequered career, whether as a youthful captain heading his boyish battalions, as leader of the revolutionary masses, or as ruler over a great city surrounded by numberless dangers, treacheries, and conspiracies, he was a stranger to timidity or irresolution. Masaniello, though amiable towards all, was nevertheless respected. Sincere and honest, he was often called upon to arbitrate between those of his own class who were disputants. He seemed born to contribute to the good of others and to the greatness of his country rather than to his own, for no one was ever more humble in power, more magnanimous, more incorruptible, or more zealous in

* Gabriele Tontoli, "Il Masaniello," p. 123.

† Baldacchini, "Storia Napoletana," p. 25.

‡ Documenti degli agenti del Gran Duca di Toscana. Lettere del Cardinal Filomarino. Archivio Storico Italiano, vol. ix.

doing good.* Never under his singular changes of fortune did he desire to repudiate the popular mode of living or manners, or to throw aside the dress of his calling and originally humble position, but he steadily refused to receive titles, preferments, or rewards.† To such effect are the concurrent testimonies of historians respecting the character of Masaniello.

During the progress of the discontent excited by increased taxation under the viceroyalty of the Duke of Arcos in the year 1647, an incident occurred, which, though simple in itself, was rendered memorable by the importance of its results. Beradina, the young wife of Masaniello, was accustomed to attend the market with grain and fruits. On one occasion, having to carry a bundle of flour, she concealed it by having it abundantly wrapped as though it were a child in her arms, and hoped thus to pass the barrier unobserved into the town without payment of the ordinary duty.‡ Beradina paid a severer penalty than the toll. She was imprisoned for the attempt to evade it, and a fine of a hundred

* Botta, "Storia d'Italia," vol. vi. pp. 318—332.

† Tontoli, "Il Masaniello," pp. 94, 95.

‡ Baldacchini, "Storia Napoletana," p. 25.

ducats was levied on her husband as the cost of her liberation.*

Masaniello, who ardently loved his newly-wedded wife, left no means untried for her rescue. He was tortured by reflection as to the fate which might await Beradina, young and lovely, in the hands of lawless and merciless captors. An unquenchable fire of hatred and indignation burnt in his breast as he muttered, "Well do I know what I would do were it ever in my power." Bitter protests against the existing government escaped him when thus referring to the reforms he would effect if ever he had care of the State. The unhappy Masaniello made continual appeals to the officers of the toll, entreating them to liberate his wife. He found no pity, but his petition was met by the most insulting reply that to surrender his wife at all, even on the payment of a ransom, was more clemency than he could expect.†

Some writers affirm that the accusation against the wife of Masaniello was false, and simply a pretext for her capture. At all events, her husband

* Capecelatro, "Diario dei tumulti del popolo Napolitano," p. 14.

† Donzelli, "Partenope Liberata," p. 7.

swore solemnly to take revenge for her imprisonment. Eight days elapsed ere Masaniello could effect Beradina's release; and then not without infinite trouble and humiliating concession. The fine of a hundred ducats was extorted as Beradina's ransom, and Masaniello, in consequence, was reduced to sorer poverty than ever. The whole of his simple possessions were sold, nor would this sacrifice have been sufficient to realize the amount of the fine without assistance rendered by the charity of some who were his friends.*

Masaniello, thus made destitute, was no longer able to follow his trade as a fisherman, but was compelled to earn a still more precarious subsistence by standing in the market and selling paper for the fish to be carried in.†

The greatest of all State dramas, a revolution, is incomplete, it has been said, unless the miseries and misfortunes of a woman are mingled in it. So with the insurrection under Masaniello, it was outraged love, the tender love of a husband, the love, stronger than death, of the patriot, which led him on to a triumphant revolt. The deep sense of injury awakened in the breast of Masaniello by

* Baldacchini, "Storia Napoletana," p. 25.

† Donzelli, "Partenope Liberata," p. 6.

the treatment of his wife, was inflamed still more by the remembrance of a quarrel which had in some way arisen between him and the Duke of Maddaloni, a man odions to the people from the oppressive crnelty he exercised towards all those who were in any sense dependent upon him. Masaniello, it is affirmed, had suffered scandalous treatment from this aristocrat and the hirelings of his household.

It is possible that these occurrences first awakened the idea of conspiracy in the mind of Masaniello. Yet more probably it resulted from a long-cherished spirit of revolt against that slavery endured by the Neapolitans under its most odious aspects, beneath the tyranny of the Spanish rule in Naples. The nature of Masaniello was too noble to regard these enormities with apathy. He observed, he reflected, and he aspired. He yearned to restore the rights of his fellow-men, to champion the cause of the oppressed, and secnre to them the blessings of freedom. Heart and intellect were quickened in their action by the suffering he himself endured and the sympathy he felt for it in others.

Masaniello, though of so humble an origin, possessed a nature cast in proportions equal to his destiny, and his soul was endowed with an antique virtue. His nobility was not dwarfed by egotism, and he was truly great in proportion as he was unconsciously so. Uncompromising as Cincinnatus, he was bold as Marius, who has been judged less great for having exterminated the Cimbri than for having prostrated the aristocracy of Rome. Certain it is that from the time of Masaniello's resolve, the Revolution was inevitable.

Under Count Monterey, who had held office as viceroy of Naples from the year 1631 to 1636, the military institution had been established which had effectually trained the Popolans to the use of arms, and instructed them in the forms of war. It consisted in the organization of martial companies, divided, as we have seen, according to the quarters of the city. Each company had its *capitano*, or head, and sometimes the command of more than one company was entrusted to a single leader. These military communities possessed much the same resemblance to those which existed in the several towns of Italy during the early ages of the republics, as did, in a political sense, the Neapolitan *Sediles*, or *Seggi*, to the Florentine *Loggie*.

Masaniello was leader of several companies. Those under his command consisted for the most part of young men of his own age and of his own class.* These companies were led by their captain one day into some fields in the vicinity of Naples where stood an inn. Adjacent to it was a spring, from which the place, an exquisite spot, derived its name of *l'acqua della Bufola.*† In this pleasant solitude Masaniello could freely expound the doctrines of revolution, and discuss the arrangements necessary to the execution of his cherished project.

It was resolved that the initiative should be taken by the most youthful members of the companies, in case that, should the enterprise fail, their youth and inexperience might plead as their excuse, and also to mislead their adversaries as to the real nature of the movement. Youths and children, armed with sticks and canes, were the first insignificant elements of the Revolution.‡ The whole proceeding at its commencement was looked upon by many as a mere childish frolic, and its leader, like Brutus, was considered mad. This convenient contempt gave Masaniello leisure to mature his

* "Diario" di Capecelatro, p. 15.

† Baldacchini, "Storia Napoletana," p. 26.

‡ Ibid.

plans without hindrance. He was assisted in his designs by money from Savino Sacardo, a member of the Carmelite Order.*

In the midst of simulated extravagances many a stinging truth burst forth impetuously from the lips of Masaniello. He frequented the shops of the fruit-sellers, and took pains to excite still more the indignation created by the recently imposed tax on fruit, and protested against the cruelty which had levied it. He invited them to come in a body to the market-place, and there declare their resolve not to pay the duty. Keen-sighted people saw in all these occurrences a meaning which was not without its menace to the State; it was the agitation boding evil of the so-called "dangerous classes."

One day Masaniello, as he was returning home in a perturbed state of mind, passed the spot where Perrone—a man whose name was infamously conspicuous during the Revolution—was standing with a companion. These two men observing the perturbation of Masaniello, inquired what ailed him? He, flushed with anger, replied, "I would give my life to reform our city." To this they answered with a scoff, "You

* Donzelli, "Partenope Liberata," p. 8.

are a fine fellow, truly, to reform a city like Naples!"

"Do not jeer, my friends," retorted Masaniello, "were there but two or three of my temper you should see, by Heaven, what I could do for the good of the people." After some discussion the two men pledged their faith as adherents of Masaniello in whatever enterprise he might engage.*

The alliance was a fatal one for Masaniello, no less than for the cause he had at heart, for Domenico Perrone was a bold, bad man, audacious by nature, and without scruple where his self-interest was at stake.†

This man had escaped from prison, and to shield himself from the punishment due to his crimes, he had recourse to the nefarious practice then current in Naples, to which we have alluded, and through which those who desired to escape the civil tribunals, disguised themselves as priests. These ferocious Pharisees, protected generally by the feudal lords of the country, who, ruffians themselves, committed and connived at every conceivable atrocity, imitated their patrons in

* Giraffi, "Rivolutioni di Napoli," p. 14.

† "Diario" di Capecelatro, p. 34.

perpetrating all manner of lawless violence. This wily schemer, Perrone, though known as the Abbate Miccaro, was in reality not a priest.*

Giulio Genuino was another and equally dangerous adventurer.† He also had assumed the garb of an ecclesiastic, intent on realizing schemes more propitious to his fortunes than former adventures had proved. Genuino was of a seditious, arrogant, and turbulent temper.‡ Descended from a family not altogether obscure, he had been bred amidst civil commotions; and was well versed in persuasive arts by which to influence people and render them subservient to his own ends. He affected an ardent spirit of democracy, but possessed no genuine love of the people. He had held office as *Eletto del popolo* under the Duke of Ossuna, but in 1620 he entered into a plot, as a consequence of which he was condemned to death as guilty of high treason.§ This sentence had been commuted to perpetual imprisonment in the Castle of Orano. After the lapse of a few years he had been released, on promising to pay four thousand ducats to the King as a ransom. With

* Baldacchini, "Storia Napoletana," p. 27.

† Zazzera, "Narrazioni del governo di Duca d'Ossuna."

‡ Capecelatro, "Annali della Città di Napoli," p. 26.

§ "Diario" di Capecelatro, note viii. p. 7.

characteristic treachery Genuino ran away without paying the money. After extraordinary vicissitudes of destiny he had returned an aged man to Naples. Skilled as he was in political machinations, the influence he obtained during the turbulent times of the Revolution was immense. Unhappily his power was directed only to the basest ends. He was a traitor from the first at heart to the cause he professed to serve. Careless of the national welfare, for which he pretended enthusiasm, he resolved on ruining the man to whom he had pledged himself as a colleague. Those whom he had the misfortune to influence, he desired first to make his tools and then his victims. As he was of no creed, he was of all parties. His own interest was the single aim he had in view, regarding the national cause only as a means to the attainment of his ambition, and he desired, like Robespierre, the Revolution should end in himself. Masaniello, too confident in the faith and integrity of others, appears to have trusted him entirely. While one supported the national cause with ardour, sincerity, and intrepidity, the other secretly undermined the interests of the people by exciting them to extreme measures, and by stirring up the strife of faction, thus preventing a peaceful realization of reform. Then, at a moment favourable to his own fortunes, he threw off the disguise, forsook the public cause as it wavered in the balance, and turned in malignity against the ill-fated man whose misfortune it was to have been his associate.

CHAPTER II.

THE populace of Naples, no less than the Italian people in general, have always delighted in festivals of a religious kind. One most singularly characterized has been more sacredly observed by the Neapolitans than all others. This is the Feast of the Madonna, or Lady of Carmel, for whom they entertain a peculiar reverence.

Tradition relates how on one occasion the Turks descended on the shores of Naples, and were repulsed solely by the intervention of the Lady of Carmel. Several public celebrations took place, therefore, in her honour, and were crowned by the grand closing Feast of the Madonna, which occurred annually on the 16th of July.* A superficial fortress was then erected

* Donzelli, "Partenope Liberata," p. 7.

in the square of the market-place, where stood the temple, abundantly enriched with grateful offerings, dedicated to the gracious Lady of Carmel.* The sham castle of wood thus constructed was garrisoned by a representation of Turkish troops, who having their faces painted to imitate the Oriental tint, and clad in the Moorish garb, took the name of Alarbes, or more properly El Arbes, a term of Arabian origin, signifying the dwellers in tents. This garrison was assailed by different companies of the people under their respective leaders. The greater part consisted of the young men, who, disciplined by Masaniello, regarded him as their chief. The entire force numbered four hundred.† Their only weapons were canes or reeds, to which pitched faggots were sometimes attached for the purpose of setting fire to the Citadel.‡

The Feast of the Madonna of Carmel took place without doubt on the 16th of July. It was therefore only a rehearsal of the ceremony for which the companies under the leadership of Masaniello had assembled in the market-place on

* Gabriele Tontoli, "Il Masaniello," p. 5.

† "Diario," Capecelatro, p. 15.

‡ Gabriele Tontoli, "Il Masaniello," p. 5.

Sunday the 17th of July in the year 1647, the day signalized as the first of the Revolution. This discipline would, of course, form an essential part of the preparations for the occasion; and it was the custom, moreover, for these companies to march through the city, and pass under review on the Sundays preceding the Feast of Carmel.*

As the month of July in the year 1647 drew near, the discontent of the Neapolitans increased. The indignation of the people was inflamed into ferocity by the ruthless extortion and severity of their rulers, who were deaf to complaint and remonstrance, as they were blind to the misery and animosity around them. Despotism prevented the national feeling declaring itself through legitimate channels, and it burst forth in acts which prophesied a deadly retribution.

As early as the month of May in the memorable year 1647, a terrible conflagration, the work of unknown hands, had menaced with destruction the Spanish fleet which lay in the port at Naples. Three hundred thousand ducats were lost and four hundred soldiers perished.† The roar of the

* "Histoire des Revolutions de Naples," par le Comte de Modene, vol. i. p. 41.

† Giannone, "Storia civile di Napoli," Libro xxxvii. c. 1.

flames, which broke forth amidst the profound stillness of the night, resounded through the city, and awakened its startled inhabitants. The more thoughtful among the citizens, as they looked on the lurid glare lighting up the midnight sky, drew from it an augury of calamities to come.

On the night of the 6th of June, the Custom House in the market-place was shattered into the air by a quantity of powder secretly conveyed into it.* In the morning its blackened ruins only were seen. The meaning of the action was obvious. It signified a resolve to compel acquiescence with the general demand for a diminution of the execrated taxes. Speedily, however, a new building was erected and the Custom House established once more.

These signs of defiance on the part of the people did but render the agents of the Spanish government more insolent, overbearing, and oppressive. Through the infatuation common to tyranny in all times, the unmistakeable premonitions of revolution were disregarded, and Liberty, through this contempt of its trammelled force, gathered strength to burst its fetters and openly resist its enemies.

* Botta, "Storia d'Italia," p. 319.

Placards of seditious import were posted throughout the town, intimating that the Neapolitans would follow the example of the people of Palermo in revolt if the newly imposed tax on fruit were not removed.* Women confessed to their pastors the existence of a conspiracy in which their husbands and brothers were engaged.† The Cardinal Filomarino, when thus enlightened, gave immediate warning to the Viceroy. But the Duke of Arcos, already seized with panic, remained irresolute as to what course to pursue. History counselled him, and those who were really his friends advised him in accordance with its teachings. The people menaced and entreated alternately, but the Viceroy was insensible to all appeal.

To such a height had the public misery reached, that even many among the nobles opposed the continued imposition of the tax on fruit. It was, indeed, beyond all others odious to the people and grievously oppressive to them. In the midsummer of the warmest climate in Italy, fruit was required as a necessity and relished as a luxury. The poorer classes had

* Baldacchini, "Storia Napoletana," p. 23.

† Capecelatro, "Diario," p. 7.

been accustomed to look to it as a principal means of subsistence. They declared a tax on this article to be insupportable,* but expressed their willingness to pay increased duty were it imposed on some other provision.

Throngs gathered round the Viceroy's carriage as he proceeded to mass in the Church of the Carmelites. Fierce protests were raised against the tax, which the crowd entreated him to remove.† Peacemakers in the State advised the Duke to forbear. "Increase, rather," they said, "other burthens to the same amount, but let this alone, which will inevitably bring ruin."

On the other hand, there were not wanting counsellors of infamous cupidity who hoped to enrich themselves by conciliating the powerful and by robbing the poor. Amongst these was Andrea Naclerio, the Deputy of the people. He had also been *Eletto*, or Deputy, under the viceroyalty of the Duke of Medina, and was still retained in office, not through the choice of the Neapolitans, but through the favour of the Duke of Arcos.‡ The citizens complained sorely against

* Capecelatro, "Diario," p. 6.

† De Santis, "Historia di Napoli," p. 43.

‡ Nicolai, "Historia dell ultime Rivolutioni della città di Napoli," p. 20.

Naclerio, a man habitually harsh to the poor, and servile to those of high rank. He saw in base and mean compliances the path to emoluments and distinctions under the demoralized rule of the Spaniards in Naples, and he warmly co-operated with the Viceroy in seeking to make the people submit to the new tax.*

The discontent and disquietude which fomented in the heart of the city were echoed in the commotions which spread to its precincts. On Monday, the third day of June, whilst the Piazza Porto was assembled, an affray arose in the immediate vicinity of Naples.† Some Germans who had partaken of refreshment at a tavern refused to pay. A tumult arose, and in the midst of it some Neapolitan soldiers arrived. Three of the Germans were killed in the scufflo which ensued. Their companions took to flight and bore the news to the rest of their comrades. The Germans, thereupon, returned in a force of above a hundred, and attacked and wounded the host of the inn and his adherents. A reinforcement of Neapolitans then arrived. The contest grew hot, and was at its height when the

* Baldacchini, "Storia Napoletana," p. 20.

† "Diario" di Capecelatro, p. 8.

Spaniards, with a cowardice which had become their characteristic in the 17th century, fled in confusion to Castel Nuovo. Such was the excitement that the Piazza was broken up.

The Piazze themselves were not free from discord. Disputes among the nobles gave rise to perpetual conflicts. The citizens in the people's Piazza on May the 11th had declared their invincible repugnance to the tax on fruit. The majority of the Piazze indeed desired to repeal it. The deputies were commissioned to find some other means to meet the demands for money,* but so exhausted were all the sources of supply, that they knew not in what direction to look for a substitute for the duty on fruit.† They hesitated. Whilst they delayed the supporters of the tax, on the other hand, carried their point; and Don Carlo Spinello enjoyed a triumph which he had good reason afterwards to repent.

On Sunday morning, the 7th day of July, in the year 1647, the market-place at Naples was thronged, as usual, with sellers of fruit, laden with full baskets of their refreshing mer-

* Capecelatro, "Diario," p. 15.

† Baldacchini, "Storia Napoletana," p. 32.

chandise.* Among the vendors were the gardeners of Pozzuoli. They refused to pay the duty, saying it was the part of the Neapolitan dealers to pay; but these in their turn refused. "*Pagate voi*," "*pagate voi*," exclaimed alternately peasants and citizens. The dispute grew hot, whilst the officers of the gabelles cried impatiently, "*Sbrigatela.*" † The commotion was increased by the officers demanding five carlini for every cantaio of fruit, whereas, a few days ago, the Pozzuolans declared they had asked but three. Both citizens and peasants now openly refused to pay.

The Pozzuolans, seeing that the rapidly passing time did not increase the value of their fruits, resolved on an immediate deputation to the Viceroy.‡ These self-elected deputies were received by the Duke of Arcos with fair words, but were referred for further satisfaction of their grievances to one of the governors of the Collateral Council named Bernado Zufia. This man, whether in consequence of habitual churlishness, the ill-humour of an hour, or owing to secret instruc-

* Donzelli, "Partenope Liberata," p. 8. Botta, "Storia d'Italia," p. 320.

† Donzelli, "Partenope Liberata," p. 8.

‡ Baldacchini, "Storia Napoletana," p. 34.

tions received by him from the Viceroy, roughly dismissed the petitioners. He replied in a tone of brutality to their demands, and threatened to send them to the galleys.* Upon hearing this the suppliants rushed distractedly through the streets, crying that "Justice was exiled, and no refuge remained for the afflicted."†

Naclerio, Deputy of the people, was now commissioned by the Viceroy to repair to the market. He, not less cold-blooded than the Governor Zufia, had been heard to say, "There remain the rope and the block for the obstinate." *He* had little chance of restoring peace.

Naclerio was on the point of sailing for the enjoyment of a few days' leisure amidst the fragrant seclusions of Posilippo in company with some friends, when he received the Viceroy's command to hasten to the market-place.‡ He turned back in obedience to the order, and coasting along the shore of the Marinella, speedily reached the place of action. The excitement of the scene there was intense. The enthusiasm of the Neapolitans,

* Nicolai, "Historia dell ultime Rivolutioni di Napoli," p. 20.

† De Santis, "Historia di Napoli," p. 44.

‡ Capecelatro, "Diario," p. 17. Antonio de Tarsia, "Tumultos de la Ciudad de Napoles," p. 40.

heightened by a burning sense of injury and an invincible resolve to defy, was expressed with the ceaseless gesticulative fluency of the Improvisatore. Deputy Naclerio now maintained, as the officers had done, that it was the duty of the Pozzuolans to pay.* They replied by shouts and lamentations, and remained invincible in their determination.

Naclerio, enraged at their firmness, lost his self-command, and utterly forgetting his mission as mediator, threatened to chastise the Pozzuolans by sending them to the galleys. Still they would listen to no terms. The collectors then wished to have the fruit weighed in spite of their resistance.† The Pozzuolans at length, fairly desperate, flung down their baskets, scattering their inviting contents to the ground as they cried to the people, "Take what you can, it is the last time we will come to the market." Mad with rage, they trampled remorselessly on the exquisite fruits as they shouted, "They are ours, and we will do as we like with them."‡ The choice abundance of the Neapolitan fruit-market, from luscious pine,

* Donzelli, "Partenope Liberata," p. 9.

† Capecelatro, "Diario," p. 17.

‡ De Santis, "Historia di Napoli."

melon, pomegranate, citron, quince, and strawberry, to the fine olive and nut of Spain, lay scattered in rich masses of ripe bloom and fragrance around. Children rushed eagerly to gather up the tempting luxuries. They were rudely driven back by the "*Gaballieri*" and "*Sbirri*," and by Naclerio, who above all treated them with harshness. This conduct inflamed still more the anger of the multitude, and turned it in full force upon the Deputy. People seized the fruits on all sides as missiles of annoyance to the collectors and the detested official. Masaniello, with unerring aim, boldly dealt him a blow in the face with a handful of figs.*

The majority of the people speedily exchanged fruits for stones, which were hurled in all directions at the collectors of the tax.†

Naclerio, utterly powerless to defend himself, was in the very midst of the crowd, and at its mercy. He would in all probability never have emerged out of it had not a party of friends hastened to his rescue. After cutting a path through the multitude, with great difficulty they at length reached the spot where Naclerio stood.

* Baldacchini, "Storia Napoletana," p. 35.

† Tontoli, "Il Masaniello," p. 6.

His deliverers had then, absolutely, to bear him in their arms in order to succour him, so resolutely had the people encircled him to prevent his escape. Naclerio, rescued thus from the people's revenge, returned in safety to the palace. There, flushed with wrath and smarting with pain, he urged the Viceroy to take decisive measures against the insolent plebeians. But they, meanwhile, were gathering fresh strength for the conflict, and now from the squalid Lavinaro and the Porto, the busy Sellaria and Conciaria, as well as from all quarters of the city, the streets, and the coasts alike, fresh numbers joined the Revolution.*

The companies under Masaniello who had assembled for a mock battle were about to wage war in reality. The strategy of Masaniello had succeeded. Those who had jeered at companies of juvenile delinquents wielding no more formidable weapons than sticks and canes, now lost their false confidence, and trembled as they saw them the leaders of a vast, menacing, and tumultuous mass which threatened to overwhelm everything in its course.†

* Nicolai, "Historia dell ultime Rivolutioni di Napoli," p. 37.

† Botta, "Storia d'Italia," vol. vi. p. 321.

Naclerio having escaped the fury of the people, they turned upon the other officers of the gabelles who were present, but who speedily took to flight.* Then the multitude flocked to the Custom House, a second time the mark of destruction.† Books and documents of all kinds were destroyed very quickly, and a bright flame lit up once more the ruins of the Custom House, whilst the assembly shouted for joy. Upon this occasion the rest of the toll houses,‡ those for wearing apparel no less than those for provisions, were not spared, but afforded excellent materials for a continuous conflagration.

* Donzelli, "Partenope Liberata," p. 10.

† Baldacchini, "Storia Napoletana," p. 37.

‡ Antonio de Tarsia, "Tumultos de la Ciudad de Napoles," p. 41.

CHAPTER III.

NACLERIO having reached the palace, related to the Viceroy the proceedings at the market-place.* The Deputy did not fail, at the same time, to urge the necessity of severe measures. "If the people will not listen to the voice of authority, let them learn obedience at the cannon's mouth."†

But the Duke of Arcos had resolved on a policy of craft. Deceit was congenial to his nature. Delay suited his self-indulgent ease. Had he acted manfully, he might have secured the tranquillity of the State, the good-will of the people, and have earned an illustrious name in history. For this, courage, generosity, and

* Antonio de Tarsia, "Tumultos de la Ciudad de Napoles," p. 41.

† Baldacchini, "Storia Napoletana," p. 36.

nobility of mind were required. Don Roderigo Ponce de Leone, craven-hearted, mean, and base, possessed not one quality which does honour to mankind. To temporize, play the traitor, and act in concert with those who were assassins, was the part that the Duke of Arcos assigned to himself on the historical stage. He determined to delude the Neapolitans by a show of concession. Time would enable him to mature his machinations and extinguish effectually all hope of promised reform. The Viceroy, in order to carry out his designs, employed two comparatively popular members of the nobility, Don Tiberio Carafa and Ettore Ravaschieri, Prince of Satriano, as mediators in place of Deputy Naclerio.*

Don Tiberio Carafa especially was dear to the people, owing to his liberal and kindly nature.† Don Tiberio, infirm as he was, immediately undertook the commission, and repaired to the market-place.‡ There he sought, by the most persuasive discourse, aided by the charm of his habitually gracious bearing, to conciliate

* "Diario" di Capecelatro, p. 18.

† Donzelli, "Partenope Liberata," p. 11.

‡ Tontoli, "Masaniello," p. 16.

the people. With more zeal than discretion he promised, in the name of the Viceroy, abolition not only of the tax on fruit, but of all other imposts.*

This false movement on the part of Don Tiberio produced ere long greater tumult than ever. A declaration of universal abolition had now been voluntarily given. The multitude were eager to secure at once the boon which their rulers appeared now willing to grant. A body of four hundred of the insurrectionists accordingly surrounded Don Tiberio Carafa. He would gladly have withdrawn, but was carried on by the impatient crowd, which desired him to accompany them to St Lorenzo, the centre of the municipal authority. Their demand was incessant for the original charter granted to Naples by the Emperor Charles V. Don Tiberio, stunned by the clamour and oppressed by the heat of the crowd, felt his life to be every moment in peril. The unfortunate Prince, infirm as he was, terror-stricken and exhausted, contrived, nevertheless, to escape the living labyrinth around him. He took refuge gladly in the cell of a monk who aided his flight,† and

* "Diario" di Capecelatro, p. 19.

† De Santis, "Historia di Napoli."

making his way through a secret door repaired to Castel Nuovo. Don Tiberio subsequently fled to Rome, where, overwhelmed in mind and body, he died mad in the arms of his brother, the Cardinal Carafa.*

One impulse animated the whole body of the insurgents. This was the desire to obtain the Imperial Charter, which, practically enforced, would have prevented the introduction of fresh taxes, and would have promoted the interests of the people by increasing their votes, and by conceding to them a right of veto on all measures affecting their interests. Intent on obtaining this charter, the detachment surrounding Don Tiberio had cried, "To St Lorenzo." Absorbed by the same idea, and eager to elicit at once from the Viceroy some positive ratification of their hope, the remainder of the multitude now shouted, "To the palace, to the palace."†

Masaniello, on horseback, and holding a banner in his hand, was their leader.‡ His followers, having seized whatever weapons they could find, were armed with sticks, poles, and pikes. Miserably clad and many barefooted, utterly divested

* Capecelatro, "Diario," p. 20. † Ibid. p. 21.
‡ De Santis, "Historia di Napoli," p. 48.

of the glitter and pomp of a military procession, this singular gathering of the people presented, nevertheless, a truly formidable appearance. They were, indeed, a type of those ruthless beggars, who, whether by sea or land, were the terror of their foes; for "more terrific than the war-cry of trained bands," said old Saville of Halifax, "and the bloodiest noise in the world, is the howl of a hungry multitude and the execrations of a people infuriated by misery and wrong."

The Viceroy, ensconced in the palace, amused himself meanwhile by eating biscuits soaked in wine.* "A grievous proof it was of his misfortune to have no better entertainment for the day," writes one compassionate chronicler of the Revolution. Hearing the shouts of the approaching throng, the Viceroy looked out of the window near which he was seated.

A multitude of two thousand people,† excited and menacing, advanced with portentous tumult, rapidly and irresistibly, like the waves of a tempestuous sea. Every moment now was invaluable, and increased the imperative need for im-

* Baldacchini, "Storia Napoletana," p. 39.

† Capecelatro, "Diario," p. 20.

mediate and salutary measures on the part of the government.

The kindly Don Tiberio Carafa had entreated the Viceroy "for the love of God to ease the people's burthens, and avert the impending ruin." Cardinal Trivulzio and certain Neapolitan nobles, who now surrounded him, entreated him still.* But the Viceroy continued obdurate and regardless of their remonstrances.

Don Carlo Caracciolo, Grand Master of the Horse, had with wise foresight urged the Duke to strengthen the German Guard at the palace, but this also the Duke had failed to do.

The multitude now thronged into the courtyard. Prominent among the crowd was a man enveloped in a black cloak, whose whisper or least motion seemed to exercise an influence over the people. This was Giulio Genuino, the mock priest.†

Don Carlo Caracciolo was standing in the balcony of the palace as the revolutionists approached, shouting, "Long life to the King; down with the bad government."

"Away with the taxes" was the cry of their

* Baldacchini, "Storia Napoletana," p. 39.

† Capecelatro, "Diario," p. 20.

leader, echoed by the thousand voices of the multitude, who desired an interview with the Viceroy, but upon finding no one to give an audience,* delayed no longer their entry into the palace by force.

Don Carlo Caracciolo alone was dauntless, and resolved at once to confront the people and hear their demands. Warned of the peril he incurred, he nevertheless persisted in his determination to descend and converse with the popular leaders. Pressing with intrepidity through the crowd to the spot where Genuino was, Caracciolo endeavoured to detain him in discussion.† The populace, at first in alarm for one of their leaders, gathered closely round him, but convinced at length of Caracciolo's amicable intention, urged by a sudden impulse of reverence and gratitude, turned towards him and wanted to kiss his hands and feet. They protested against the oppressive taxes, and complained bitterly of the unwholesome bread they were compelled to eat, as placing pieces of it in his hand, they asked him whether it was food for men or for dogs?‡

* Donzelli, "Partenope Liberata," p. 12.

† Capecelatro, "Diario," p. 21.

‡ Ibid.

Caracciolo did not with indiscreet benevolence, like the Prince of Bisignano, promise total abolition of the taxes; but pledged his word to intercede with the Viceroy and see what could be done. But the time for preventive measures had past in irresolute apathy. The conduct of the Viceroy aroused distrust and engendered contempt in the hearts of the people. They were incredulous of promises which they plainly saw had been extorted through fear, and they despised the cowardice out of which they sprang. If the people had hitherto felt their *right* to resist, they were now conscious for the first time of their *power* to oppose.

The tumult continued to increase as fresh numbers joined the revolutionists, crying "Into the palace, into the palace!" Caracciolo, convinced that it was useless to attempt to negotiate, upon finding all his efforts to conciliate were in vain, hastened to forestall the resolve of the multitude. He enjoined the Viceroy in a secret message to escape as swiftly as possible to Castel Nuovo.*

The gate of the palace was held by the German Guard, who in their endeavour to de-

* "Diario" di Capecelatro, p. 22.

fend it were speedily overcome. Their arms were taken from them, and many were wounded in the contest. The Spanish Guard made no resistance to the triumphant populace.* The wisdom of Caracciolo's advice to strengthen the military forces was now proved. The revolutionists met with no organized resistance whatever, and the Spanish and the German soldier, whose valour had often turned the tide of victory on European battle-fields, alike gave way before those relentless adversaries whom Deputy Naclerio had termed "the insolent plebeians."

Having forced their way up the great staircase of the palace, they assailed the reception rooms.† The door of the first was broken in with repeated blows from an iron club.

Caracciolo, who had re-entered the palace, endeavoured once more to appease the fury of the people. He could no longer interfere with impunity. A reckless blow with an iron weapon was aimed at his head; but he, dexterously warding it, received only a slight wound in the arm. Caracciolo, then closing with his assailants,

* Baldacchini, "Storia Napoletana," p. 22. Tontoli, "Il Masaniello," p. 10.

† Baldacchini, "Storia Napoletana," p. 38.

got possession of the iron stave. He wished to draw his sword, but the crowd hissed and bade him give back the stave if he would use his sword. But the valiant Caracciolo could neither wield his sword nor keep the stave, for he was just then struck and disabled by the stones with which he was pelted by some in the crowd.*

The people continued to lament and declaim with unmeasured wrath against Naclerio, whom they wished to have deposed. Meanwhile the Deputy, who was within the palace, concealed himself with a cowardice equal to that of his Ducal patron, in the apartments of the Vice-Duchess. Then, taking advantage of the first propitious moment, he let himself down by a rope from a window which looked out on the adjacent park. He then repaired to Castel Nuovo.†

The Viceroy on receiving Caracciolo's message endeavoured to follow the example of Naclerio. Descending by a secret winding staircase‡ of the palace which led into the court-yard, he made his way thence into the square, with the idea that the entire multitude had entered the

* Capecelatro, "Diario," p. 22.

† De Santis, "Historia di Napoli," p. 50.

‡ Antonio de Tarsia, "Tumultos de la Ciudad de Napoles," p. 46.

palace. In this he was deceived, for he was immediately surrounded.* With difficulty he freed himself from the throng, and jumped into a coach, into which he was invited by Don Antonio de Taboada, who happened to be passing at the time.†

A single champion, however, would not have sufficed for the Viceroy's rescue. Fortunately for him, some nobles of the court, the Marquis of Torrecuso, Don Emmanuel Vaez, and Carlo Caracciolo, succeeded in making way through the crowd to his assistance. Their succour was needed. The revolutionists surrounded the Viceroy's carriage, and one of them made a thrust with his sword at the Duke.‡ The blow was parried by Don Emmanuel Vaez, who was afterwards created Grand Master of the Horse by the Viceroy in reward for this service. Confusion increased as the harness was torn from the horses and the driver dragged off the box. The harness was recovered by two of the nobles, who fastened it on the horses, while the rest formed a guard round the carriage. The intrepid Caracciolo again mounted the coach, and sought to pursue with it the desired course.

* Donzelli, "Partenope Liberata," p. 12.

† Capecelatro, "Diario," p. 23.

‡ Baldacchini, "Storia Napoletana," p. 41.

But it seemed fruitless to attempt to proceed. The noise, the confusion, and the dense crowd, rendered this next to impossible. The carriage was swayed backwards and forwards as the multitude pressed hither and thither.* The Duke of Arcos, thinking to facilitate his escape, continually threw handfuls of small coin out of the carriage window.† But the people would not be bribed. Voices in the crowd cried, "We are poor, it is true, but we are not to be silenced or sent away by money. Take off the taxes: this is what we want." ‡

Caracciolo found it impossible to make progress, but possessing promptitude as well as valour, he instantly resolved upon an expedient. He justly feared for the life of the Viceroy, should he not speedily be enabled to reach his intended destination—the convent of St Louis. Dismounting hastily, he made the Duke descend also from the carriage, and seizing him by the arm, while the other nobles raised their swords in a circle of defence and warded off the pressure of the crowd, he cried, "Give place to the King." The words acted like a spell on the people, who in-

* Baldacchini, "Storia Napoletana," p. 41.

† De Santis, "Historia di Napoli," p. 51.

‡ Donzelli, "Partenope Liberata," p. 12.

stantly fell back, and allowed Caracciolo to pass on.* One of the multitude only, more audacious than the rest, rushed on the Viceroy, and seizing him by the hair, partially stunned him with a blow as he cried, "Away with the taxes."

It is not credible that the multitude believed in the actual presence of the monarch of Spain; but they were impressed by this allusion to their sovereign, and were submissive for the moment under a returning sense of obedience to constitutional authority. The people remained faithful at heart in their allegiance to the sovereign of Spain as head of the government, and sought release only from the lawless and oppressive rule which represented the court of Madrid in Naples, and were the righteous enemies of a local administration which had rendered itself odious by committing every kind of despotic enormity. Hence the perpetual cry of the Revolution to its close, "Long life to the monarch of Spain. Death to the bad government. Away with the taxes!" An appeal to the sentiment of loyalty, therefore, possessed an all-powerful influence. This fact is sufficient to redeem the memory of Masaniello and his adherents from the imputation of reckless and sanguinary

* Capecelatro, "Diario," p. 24.

revolt, with which superficial encyclopædists have not scrupled to charge them. Nay, more, it constitutes the Revolution of the year 1647, a noble effort for political redemption, and elevates its leader into a rank with those whose names are most illustrious in the History of Reform.

Through the strategy of Caracciolo, the Viceroy succeeded in reaching the convent of St Louis. But the gates were found shut, and the terrified monks had no desire to open them. After repeated demands, the portals were at length partly unclosed, when the indomitable Caracciolo hastily pushed the Viceroy within, and then effected his deliverance.*

The company of nobles who had been the Viceroy's escort remained without, at the mercy of the angry crowd infuriated at the escape of the Duke of Arcos. The Marquis of Brienza was wounded, and Caracciolo saved himself with difficulty.

Meanwhile, a work of destruction was going on at the palace, which was now in the hands of the revolutionists. The costly contents of this ducal habitation were remorselessly destroyed, and hurled out of the crashing windows, to min-

* Capecelatro, "Diario."

ble with the refuse of the roads.* When the halls and saloons were thoroughly dismantled, the edifice itself was attacked, and its lighter and ornamental portions either disfigured or totally demolished.† The documents of the Secretary of the Chamber, and those of the writers of the seal, were torn into fragments, and scattered to the four winds.

In the midst of this general wreck of palatial luxury, singular respect was shown for the possessions of Cardinal Trivulzio, who had interceded with the Viceroy for the repeal of the tax on fruit. Not a single article in his apartments at the palace was sacrificed.‡ It is well that the Neapolitans, whilst wreaking vengeance upon their foes, did not forget the gratitude due to a benefactor.

* Nicolai, "Historia del ultime Rivolutioni di Napoli," p. 25. Donzelli, "Partenope Liberata," p. 11.

† Capecelatro, "Diario," p. 23.

‡ Giraffi, "Istoria di Sollevazioni di Napoli," p. 25.

CHAPTER IV.

Among the few names which are honourably distinguished in connection with the Neapolitan Revolution, is that of the Cardinal Ascanio Filomarino, a prelate who appears to have been much and deservedly loved by the people of Naples. As early as the 7th of July, in the year 1647, we find him an active participator in the events of the hour, taking the part of mediator* between contending classes, and adopting with energy and intrepidity the only course consistent with his vocation and character.†

As the Cardinal in his carriage was on his way to the convent of the Capuchins, he was informed

* Antonio de Tarsia, "Tumultos de la Ciudad de Napoles," p. 46.

† Lettere del Cardinal Filomarino. Archivio Storico Italiano, vol. ix.

of the tumult which had arisen. He was warned repeatedly to return to his house. Familiar friends whom he met entreated him to discontinue his course. No one could answer for consequences, even where the popular pastor of Naples was concerned. Paolo Emilio, physician to the Cardinal, especially endeavoured to dissuade him from exposing himself to such evident risk.* The Cardinal answered, "I was obedient to your counsel, and you did your duty, despising danger when I was sick, and now when I am well, let me also do my duty as a true pastor and father of my people."†

The Cardinal then sent back his little nephew who was with him, and passed on hastily towards the palace.‡ Here the presence of armed tumultuous masses corroborated the news he had received. As he reached the square, his carriage was surrounded. The Cardinal, with a kindly greeting to the people, gave them his blessing, saying, "He had always found them full of respect and affection for their pastor." The venerable aspect of the Cardinal soothed and reassured the

* Capecelatro, "Diario," p. 25.

† Burana, "Batalla Peregrina," p. 20.

‡ Donzelli, "Partenope Liberata," p. 11.

people. They wept and entreated. "They could not endure," they declared, "such oppression, and they had no faith in the promises of the Viceroy."

The Cardinal replied by promising to seek redress for their wrongs, and assured them that he was ready to shed his blood on their behalf. As Filomarino proceeded fresh crowds pressed around him, until in order to enable him to pursue his course, it became necessary for one of the popular leaders to remain at his side and make way for him, by exhorting the multitude to moderation.

Filomarino arrived after much difficulty in the immediate vicinity of the monastery where the Viceroy was sheltered. Finding it impracticable, however, to obtain an interview with the Duke, the Cardinal sent Cesare Gheradini, his chamberlain, to inform the Viceroy of what had passed.*

The Duke of Arcos in reply sent a written declaration, expressing his willingness to concede whatever the Neapolitans desired.† This document was conveyed to the Cardinal by the

* Capecelatro, "Diario," p. 25.

† Baldacchini, "Storia Napoletana," p. 43.

Marquis of Torrecuso, who, with some other nobles less valiant than Carracciolo, had succeeded in gaining access into the monastery through a secret passage.

The declaration forwarded to the Cardinal by the Viceroy promised a universal abolition of the taxes. It was read by Filomarino to the people, who in gratitude kissed his hands and his clothes.* This demonstration on the part of the people is to be regarded rather as an expression of attachment towards one whom they looked upon as a friend and benefactor, than as a token of satisfaction with the document. The fact of having obtained it produced no abiding influence whatever, for it was distrusted like every other concession accorded by the Viceroy.

The insurrection proceeded unchecked. The Spanish guard at the lower gate of the palace was attacked. Their arms were seized, their drums broken, their standards torn out of the hands of the bearers, and their muskets taken.† The Spaniards, exasperated at this indignity, fired a sharp volley, which descended

* Lettere del Cardinal Filomarino. Archivio Storico Italiano, vol. ix.

† Nicolai, "Historia del ultime Rivolutioni di Napoli," p. 28.

fatally on more than one of the multitude.* The first of those who was struck down was reverenced as a martyr by the revolutionists, who carried the body of their fallen compatriot in a mourning procession through the city. No hero of antiquity sacrificed to his country could have been followed with greater veneration than was this obscure member of the populace by the Neapolitans. The streets resounded with lamentations, and women with their cries and tears excited their lovers, husbands, and brothers to revenge.† Animosity was kindled afresh in the hearts of the citizens, and a fearful clamour arose. The populace had a bitter revenge. Turning fiercely upon the Spanish and German guard, who fell killed and wounded in all directions, the numerous foreign soldiery in Naples, now thoroughly intimidated, either hid themselves in the monasteries or whatever other refuges they could find, or fraternized with the revolutionists.‡ Many of the troops quitted their posts in the public way, and took to flight, some of them

* Capecelatro, "Diario," p. 26.

† Baldacchini, "Storia Napoletana," p. 42.

‡ Nicolai, "Historia del ultime Rivolutioni di Napoli," p. 28. Baldacchini, "Storia Napoletana," p. 42. Donzelli, "Partenope Liberata," p. 12.

retiring to a portion of the palace grounds nearest to Castel Nuovo.

The Viceroy, taking advantage of the moment when the presence of Cardinal Filomarino diverted the attention of the people, escaped through a back door of the monastery into a garden leading to the slope of the Pizzofalcone rock. Here, in company with those nobles who had remained with him in his flight, he took up his abode in an adjacent habitation until a sedan chair was procured to facilitate his escape to more strongly fortified quarters. A portion of the necessary journey lay over a steep mountain tract, and such was the weight of the corpulent occupant of the chair, that the bearers of it could not proceed. The Duke was compelled to alight, and, panting with heat and fatigue, had to climb the remainder of the height on foot,* in order to reach the castle of St Elmo, which lies beyond the bridge, uniting the hill of Pizzofalcone to that of San Martino. St Elmo, destitute of provisions and ammunition, was in no condition to withstand a lengthened siege.† The Duke of Arcos, therefore, gave orders to the custodians of the castle for its

* De Santis, "Storia di Napoli."

† Baldacchini, "Storia Napoletana," p. 46.

increased security, and proceeded under cover of the midnight darkness to Castel Nuovo,* which, owing to its central position, its vicinity to the sea, and its conjunction with the Royal Palace, presented the most available point for intrenchment. In case of continuance in command, the heart of the city constituted the appropriate seat of government; in case of the Viceroy's deposition, the sea afforded the most convenient mode of flight.

The foreign troops, including the guards of the palace and those who had quitted their posts in the Spanish quarter, were now concentrated in the park adjacent to the castle, under command of the Prince of Ascoli.†

The Viceroy had been met during his flight from the monastery by Francesco di Somma, brother of the Prince of Colle. Francesco di Somma followed the cavalcade to its first destination at St Elmo. Here decrees were drawn up to convoke the People's Piazza. Total abolition of the taxes and the deposition of deputy Naclerio were again promised. These decrees were entrusted to Francesco di Somma to forward to the

* Tontoli, "Il Masaniello," p. 25.

† Capecelatro, "Diario," p. 27.

Governor Zufia and to Giuseppe Palmisano, secretary of the People's Piazza. But Governor Zufia, knowing well the animosity he had excited among the revolutionists, was so fearful of their revenge, that nothing could induce him to come forth from his hiding-place, even to have an audience of Di Somma. All he would do was to write an order to Secretary Palmisano. He, too, panic-stricken, had hidden himself so effectually, that although the indefatigable Francesco employed the greater part of the night in the search, he could not find him.* Into such incapable and irresolute hands had the administration fallen.

The revolutionists, having disarmed the foreign soldiery and obtained possession of the palace, proceeded to open the prisons, commencing with that of St Giacomo.† "Let us release all who are imprisoned for the taxes," they exclaimed. The inmates of the prison of the Vicarial Court alone were not liberated.‡ Here a strong guard was kept by the officers of the court and the *Sbirri*, not so much to ensure the safe custody of the prisoners, as for the preservation of the valu-

* Capecelatro, "Diario," p. 27.

† Botta, "Storia d'Italia," vol. vi. p. 321.

‡ Tontoli, "Il Masaniello," p. 25.

able Archives of the Royal Patrimony, which were there. The prisoners, finding themselves disappointed in their hopes of emancipation by the revolutionists, tried to become their own liberators.* They were shot down in the attempt, and two of them were killed. The reverence entertained by the Neapolitans for every institution established by the Emperor Charles V. accounts for their not having shown the least desire to assail the prison of the Vicarial.

The toll houses in the city, meanwhile, were demolished.† The revolutionists were anxious to obliterate everywhere the symbols of oppressive and illegal extortion. As the night of the 7th approached, a terrible tumult prevailed. Whilst in the Castel Nuovo ministers and nobles consulted how to subdue the insurrection, its leaders at the market-place stimulated their followers to a determined resistance. Incendiary fires lighted up the city, and around the sacrificial ruins of property hovered with savage satisfaction the half-clad, wretched inhabitants of the poorer districts of Naples. Genuino, the mock priest,

* Donzelli, "Partenope Liberata," p. 14.

† Antonio de Tarsia, "Tumultos de la Ciudad de Napoles," p. 41.

masked and enveloped in his black garments, glided perpetually like a shadow of ill omen at the side of Masaniello.

Processions of the Jesuits, the Theatines, and the various monastic communities in Naples traversed the most populous quarters in the direction of the market-place, praying and exhorting the people, who in answer to their devotional entreaties insulted and reviled them. The Jesuits, who, it was said, committed many acts contrary to monastic rule, were especially the object of popular derision. "It is universally known," muttered the angry multitude, "what rich lands and estates are swallowed up by you, and what benefits and luxuries you enjoy at the expense of the people. Let every one judge how much such possessions and pomp become those who profess to be religious and pious men." Under mockeries such as these the monks continued their course for awhile, but on approaching the market-place they could proceed no further. "Go, fathers," screamed the people, now openly menacing them, "go, and make orations in your temples. You made no processions hitherto in order that we might not be afflicted and oppressed with fresh taxes, but now that there is a talk of repealing them, you come and deafen us with your chants. Go and pray; it will be the best work you can do." *

Then from the various churches arose a solemn prayer for the return of peace to the agitated city. But the echo of the *Ora pro Nobis* was distinct only at intervals amidst the clamour and shouts of the excited multitude.

* De Santis, "Historia di Napoli," p. 56.

CHAPTER V.

The tumult which had prevailed during the night of the 7th of July did not abate with the approaching dawn. As the day advanced thousands were marching through the town. The air resounded with their cries, which mingled with the din of drums and trumpets and the clash of arms. Swords and lances glittered in the sunlight and martial colours flaunted in the summer breeze.* The revolution of a day had changed the entire aspect of the city. The peaceful pursuits of industry were abandoned. Mechanics and artisans rallied round the standard of revolt. Even at this early date, the true body of the Neapolitan people, the working classes, took part in the insurrection.†

* Giraffi, "Rivolutioni di Napoli," p. 39.

† Tontoli, "Il Masaniello," p. 11. "Diario" di Capecelatro.

Peasants from the rural districts, armed with pitchforks, scythes, and spades, or whatever rude weapons of warfare they could command, flocked to the city.* Despatches were sent along the coast from Pozzuoli to Salerno, summoning the inhabitants of Santa Lucia and Chiaia to take oath of allegiance to the Revolution, under penalty of seeing their lands burnt around them. Numbers of women even were seen armed, and as in the motley throngs led on by the Knights of the Cross, youths and girls of tender years united to form a second Child's Crusade.

As the Revolution progressed, the people acquired an ample supply of fire-arms. They hastened, in order to secure them, to storm the public and private repositories of military stores. Those in charge of the magazines and arsenals refused at their peril to surrender. A report spread that a quantity of powder lay in a house at the Molo Piccolo. Thither the insurgents hastened. The owner of the powder refused to surrender it, but unable to resist the furious impetuosity of the crowd, he had to fly for his life. The insurgents entered his habitation, and were about to take possession of the desired booty, when a single act

* Giraffi, "Rivolutioni di Napoli," p. 39.

of imprudence gave rise to a fearful calamity. A lighted match was incautiously brought to the spot and ignited the powder. With a terrible crash the house flew in fragments through the air.* Forty-five persons were instantly killed, and a greater number were maimed and wounded by the falling masonry scattered in all directions around.† Then the repository under the charge of Battista Buzzacherino, a Genoese, and government contractor, was assailed. Fortunately for Buzzacherino, he did not hesitate to fly in haste from his post at the approach of danger. The stores of powder had been wetted in obedience to orders received from government. Incensed at this discovery, the people would doubtless have wreaked the full force of their anger on the unfortunate Genoese personally, but in his absence they contented themselves with the ransack of his house and the destruction of his possessions.‡

Encouraged by these successes, the revolutionists resolved upon the important conquest of St Lorenzo. Owing to the advantageous position of this fortress in the upper portion of Naples, St

* Antonio de Tarsia, "Tumultos de la Ciudad de Napoles," p. 61.

† De Santis, "Historia di Napoli," p. 60.

‡ Baldacchini, "Storia Napoletana," p. 47.

Lorenzo constitutes one of the most important points of the city. The historical associations of centuries cluster round this ancient Franciscan monastery originally dedicated to the holy Saint Lawrence. Here the parliaments were held under the stormy rule of the Angevins, and in its Gothic-roofed chapter-house, adorned with arabesques and pictures of saints and priests, the deputies of the town had been accustomed to assemble. As the seat of the municipal government, here too was placed the public artillery, and here was deposited the much-desired ancient Charter of the City. The revolutionists desired ardently to become the masters of this noble edifice, politically and religiously sacred in their eyes. Its conquest would ensure to them not only the possession of a commanding military post, but also the arms and archives of the city. St Lorenzo, like St Elmo, was in no condition to withstand a siege by a stout detachment of the revolutionists, whose numbers rapidly augmented. St Lorenzo was garrisoned only by a small body of troops under the command of Don Carlo Capecelatro, who was no unworthy descendant of one of the most illustrious among the Neapolitan noble families.

The Viceroy at the eleventh hour bethought

himself of the importance attaching to the place, and of the mischief which would result from its acquisition by the people. The public documents were accordingly conveyed to the monastery of St Paul. Orders had also been given to spike the cannon and to spoil the ammunition, but these instructions were but partially carried out, and did not prevent the people from turning the powder to good account as soon as it fell into their hands.* The Viceroy now sent a slender reinforcement of Spanish troops under command of Biagio di Fusco.

During the first attack made by the revolutionists on St Lorenzo, a sharp fire poured incessantly upon them, and they were for awhile effectually repulsed.† Though repelled, they were not intimidated, but speedily returned in greater numbers and animated by greater fury.‡ The terrified monks had fled in dismay from the infuriated masses, who branded them as cowards and traitors for having caused the Spaniards to enter.§

Upon the second assault of the fortress the insurgents were momentarily driven back, but

* Capecelatro, "Diario," p. 31.

† De Santis, "Historia di Napoli."

‡ Capecelatro, "Diario," p. 44.

§ Donzelli, "Partenope Liberata," p. 26.

effected an entrance into the monastery through a gate which led from an adjacent unfrequented passage to the cloisters. The encounter which ensued was fierce on both sides. A sharp volley took place, but the people with deafening shouts pressed on the conflict in such numbers and with such irresistible impetus, that the slender garrison was completely overwhelmed, and victory speedily declared itself on the side of the insurgents. A handkerchief waved by the Spaniards from the venerable tower of the monastery in token of capitulation proclaimed St Lorenzo in the hands of the revolutionists. Valuable arms were thus acquired. Thirteen pieces of artillery, including some cannon of remarkable size, fell into the hands of the victors, in addition to a quantity of ammunition. The revolutionists, overjoyed at the victory, ascended the tower of the monastery and displayed the national banner from its heights. The great bell of the Campanile, which had so often summoned the citizen militia to arms, rang out loud peals of revolutionary triumph. The people had reason to feel proud of this important victory, glorious in itself and still more honourable to the victors, owing to the magnanimity displayed by them towards the vanquished. The Spaniards having surrendered, were spared all further suffering and ignominy, and were sent in freedom to the Viceroy.

The conquest of St Lorenzo was followed by fresh successes. A body of four hundred German troops, on their way to Naples from Torre del Greco, and a company of six hundred coming from Pozzuoli, were met and disarmed by the people.* The detachment coming from Torre del Greco, terrified at the first sight of Masaniello and his numerous followers, fled in dismay, and at length took shelter in a church of the Augustines in the street of the White Stone.† Masaniello upon arriving at the spot addressed the fugitives in friendly terms, promising not to injure them if they would open the doors of the church. This they refused to do, upon which the doors were fired, when the insurgents entering, speedily disarmed the troops and led them captive to the city. As they appeared in a starving condition, they were by Masaniello's order abundantly fed, and upon their swearing not to take arms against the popular party, were set at liberty, under the strict conditions that they were to remain within a certain quarter of the city.

* De Santis, "Historia di Napoli," p. 74.

† Donzelli, "Partenope Liberata," p. 27.

As the Revolution advanced, and even as early as the second day of its progress, the respectable portion of the populace, that is to say, the working classes, did not hesitate to declare themselves on the side of the insurgents.* This did not prevent the mass of the multitude from committing those excesses which appear the inevitable accompaniments of insurrection. In proportion to the pressure, so is the recoil, and the necessary reaction from centuries of bondage and suffering, when the people of Naples became triumphant, was a foreshadowing of that reign of Terror which somewhat more than a century later desolated France.

The revolutionists were eager to destroy in all quarters the evidences of illegal exactions, and to testify by an unsparing wreck of everything merely material in value, their detestation of the rapacity of those who, ruling over them feudally and officially, had been enriched through extortion and plunder, those who, to use the proverbial phrase of the revolutionists, "had drank the blood of the people."† Thus, sumptuous household furniture, rich tissues, gold and

* Capecelatro, "Diario," p. 34.

† Baldacchini, "Storia Napoletana," p. 52.

silver plate of exquisite workmanship, costly ornaments, cabinets of curiosities, rare jewels, and precious stones, were relentlessly amassed in sacrificial heaps for burning.*

The houses most ruthlessly ransacked were those of the nobility, the officers of the gabelles, and the government agents, who were regarded by the people as their oppressors and the objects of a just execration.

The system of farming the tolls in Naples had given rise to the most monstrous evils. In the case of extraordinary taxes, the capital was sold, and the mode of obtaining the money was left to the ingenuity or unscrupulousness of the purchaser; whilst in the case of the ordinary taxes the proceeds themselves were farmed. It will easily be seen how ruinous and oppressive to the people was the effect of these involved monetary relations, leaving an arbitrary power in the hands of irresponsible agents, by whom oftener than not it was made an excuse for the most audacious and cruel extortion. Farming the tolls was a business carried on chiefly by foreigners who had settled in Naples, and especially by the Genoese, who

* Botta, "Storia d'Italia," vol. vi. p. 321. Capecelatro, "Diario," p. 52.

exhibited above every other mercantile nation of Italy the sordid instincts of the true money-trader. A very large proportion of the pecuniary transactions of the Neapolitan State was engrossed by the Genoese, and a bitter animosity existed against them in the heart of the Neapolitan people. The Revolution of the year 1647 did not fail to bring a crushing retribution upon all the farmers of tolls, amongst whom the Genoese occupied a prominent place.

Girolamo Letizia, farmer of the gabelle on flour, was the first to suffer, and to suffer severely. The whole of his property was hurled into the streets and given to the flames. A heap of ashes was soon all that remained of the sumptuous contents of his habitation.*

Not less fiercely did the revolutionists attack the abode of Counsellor Antonio Angelis, surnamed in derision "counsellor of bad counsel," for having assisted in imposing the fresh tax on fruit. This man, originally of the humblest fortunes, had been enriched at the expense of the people.† He, too, had been *Elect* of the people in the time of the Duke of Monterey, and like so

* Baldacchini, "Storia Napoletana," p. 52.

† De Santis, "Historia di Napoli," p. 64.

many other subservient *Eletti* under the viceregal *régime*, he had been rewarded for his ingenuity in ill-doing and his servility in complying with the ministerial demands. He even boasted publicly of the facility with which, through unsparing exactions, he had raised the donatives, and of the rewards which he had in consequence obtained. This most upright of Royal Counsellors still aspired to the higher post of the Governorship of Chancery, which, as one of the most important state offices, had been usually acceded only to those of distinguished ability and merit. The possessions of Counsellor Angelis were costly in the extreme. These, piled in sumptuous masses, were burnt in front of the noble palace he had erected for himself without the Porta Reale.* Thus were forfeited the ill-gotten gains he had received at the hands of the Viceroy in recompense for the rigour with which he had imposed the burthen of taxation on the poor.

The haughty Counsellor Miraballo was accused of the same offences, and met with the same treatment. With eager fury the revolutionists then sought the house of Naclerio, the hated Deputy, who was not forgotten in the revenge

* Donzelli, "Partenope Liberata," p. 18.

which the people took on their oppressors. But the crafty Naclerio had outwitted his pursuers. Anticipating the treatment which awaited him, he had taken flight from his accustomed residence, but not ere he had done his best to secure the gorgeous riches of its contents by concealing them in the Monastery of Santa Maria della Sanita. His house was found empty. Only the delicious gardens and grounds, fragrant with choicest flowers and brilliant with glittering fountains and marble glories which would have done honour to the palace of a king, remained with the mansion itself for the people to demolish. There was no reprieve for the man whom they had so mercilessly pelted with stones at the market-place, and soon a devouring flame was kindled which speedily laid waste the magnificent abode.*

The house of Alfonso Valenzano, a farmer of the gabelle on flour, was also sacked.† But Valenzano, like Naclerio, had foreseen the coming visitation, and endeavoured also to save his property by concealing it. But the insurgents now suspected the expedient, and not finding the

* Baldacchini, "Storia Napoletana," p. 53.

† Nicolai, "Historia del ultime rivolutioni di Napoli," p. 39.

possessions of Valenzano so costly as they had anticipated, made diligent search till the hidden accumulations of money, jewels, and valuables were discovered. The jewels were of the most costly description, but these, like everything else, were unsparingly given to the flames.*

The streets and squares of Naples blazed in different directions with these gorgeous ruins. Yet it is to be remembered, to the honour of the people, that the acts of incendiarism were not committed for the purpose of self-aggrandizement. Not a single article was appropriated.† When one of the multitude wished to retain a simple chain of gold he was bitterly reproved by his companions. "Would you," they cried, "sully the glory of a noble action by a paltry theft, and let the world say we have shown ourselves robbers rather than reformers?"‡ After this, so zealous were the revolutionists to maintain the honour of their cause, that a proclamation was issued, decreeing that under penalty of death no one should seize or preserve a single article.

The night of the 8th closed in amidst scenes

* Baldacchini, "Storia Napoletana," p. 53.

† Botta, "Storia d'Italia," vol. vi. p. 321.

‡ Donzelli, "Partenope Liberata," p. 13.

of desolation and dismay, which, as an eminent historian of the insurrection observes, "lead us to conclude that punishment is sent at length for crime."

CHAPTER VI.

THE Rebellion of a Day, unchecked in its course, sufficed to convince the Viceroy of the utter inefficiency of his resources for its suppression. It was no humane motive which caused him to repudiate an immediate appeal to arms; but he felt it to be infatuation to rely on forces which were hourly proved to be inadequate to contend against the vast body of the people in arms. He hesitated, therefore, to take severe measures.* Not without personal risk, moreover, could he chastise as rebels those who incessantly expressed their devotion to royal authority and their desire to remain obedient to lawful rule. Interest and inclination alike prompted a policy

* De Santis, "Historia di Napoli," p. 67. Baldacchini, "Storia Napoletana," p. 50.

of subtlety and fraud on the part of the Duke of Arcos. Those who could not be vanquished by open force might be conquered by secret perfidy. A show of concession would ensure virtual triumph, and promises were lavishly given which were intended to be lawlessly violated. The measures of the Duke of Arcos continued in accord with his character to be those of the fox rather than of the lion.

The Viceroy having resolved upon the expedient of seemingly pacific measures, selected as an envoy to negotiate with the people, the noble Prince of Montesarchio, the descendant of an ancestry whose brilliant martial fame had for centuries rendered the name of D'Avalos not not less renowned than the names of Pescara and Del Vasto. Montesarchio rode to the marketplace armed with despatches, declaring full concession to whatever the people demanded.* But his mission had not the slightest effect in quieting the assembled multitude, who persisted in disbelieving the authenticity of the document.†

Ettore Ravascheri, the Prince of Satriano, and the Prince Bisignano, knights who had been

* Donzelli, "Partenope Liberata," p. 26.

† Capecelatro, "Diario," p. 34.

honoured with the illustrious order of the Golden Fleece, were the next Deputies employed.* They, with their hands on the sacred book in the church of the Carmelites, promised on the part of the Viceroy total repeal of the taxes.† To all these declarations the people replied by a single sentence obdurately repeated, "The Document is false."

So far, attempts at negotiation had proved fruitless. The Duke of Arcos, baffled and perplexed, had recourse to a measure which, whatever might have been the motive from which it sprang, proved signally disastrous in its consequences. The habitual usage of the Viceroys, when critically circumstanced, was to foment existing feuds by exciting still greater discord between the aristocracy and the poorer classes. The jealousy of the viceroys concerning the power and influence possessed by the nobles was appeased when they saw the popular ill-will turned against them. The selection by the Duke of Arcos of one as a Deputy who was known to be odious to the people supports this idea. Only the supposition of positive infatuation, or the deepest du-

* Giraffi, "Rivolutioni di Napoli," p. 45.
† Baldacchini, "Storia Napoletana," p. 50.

plicity on the part of the Viceroy, can account for the fact of his having made choice of Diomed Carafa as a mediator.

Diomed Carafa, Duke of Maddaloni, was a descendant of that Diomed, first count of Maddaloni, whose bold ambition had laid in the 15th century the foundation of the future wealth and power of his race. Count Diomed of Maddaloni had inherited the courage of his ancestors—those valorous Dukes of Naples, one of whom was forced, nevertheless, to yield in the 12th century, after heroic resistance, the last Grecian free state of Italy to the indomitable Normans. This Diomed Carafa it was, who, devoted to the House of Arragon, had assisted in the conquest of Naples, in the year 1442, by introducing the Spaniards into the town through an aqueduct; and who, at a later date, performed no less signal service to Spain by supporting the cause of Royalty, when menaced by the war of the Barons. Among the rewards granted by the Spanish monarch to Carafa, in return for his services, was the fiefdom of Maddaloni. Upon the slope of the Apennines, to the north of Naples, stands, commanding a noble prospect over sea and plain, the ruin of the ancient castle of Maddaloni. A lofty watch tower, one or two stray turrets, and a wall, form the picturesque fragments, from which the traveller would infer but little of the significance of the structure during the feudal days, or the momentous part enacted by its owners in the history of Naples. The lapse of two centuries, from the time of the Spanish invasion of Naples, saw the Carafas in possession of a power equalling that of the most potent rulers in Europe, for not even the Imperial sanction was sued for when the venerable Cardinal Carafa, at the age of seventy-six, assumed the dignity of the successors of St Peter, as Paul IV. A century later, and the stormy annals of the house of Maddaloni had recorded the downfall and ignominious doom of three of the Carafa lineage, till, in the year 1647, the revolution prepared for another Diomed Carafa an equally disastrous end. In the 17th century the Carafas still remained devoted to the Spanish interest. Through intermarriages with the noblest families, their wealth and influence had been augmented. They commanded vast resources, and held sway over an almost unlimited number of vassals. With such means at their disposal, and inheriting the fierce passions and unscrupulous ambition of their race, it was not surprising that the brothers, Diomed and Giuseppe Carafa, should have been dishonourably distinguished above others of the depraved aristocracy of Naples, for the audacious lawlessness, licence, and tyranny which characterized the majority of their class. Giuseppe Carafa was accused of the gravest crimes; and to such a height had Don Diomed carried his extortion and imperious violence towards his feudatories, and the Neapolitans in general, that he was at length imprisoned in the Castel Nuovo.* Don Diomed, a patron of banditti and a leader of reprobates, was secretly an intimate associate of the base Perrone, the one an enemy to the commonwealth of which he was a member, the other a traitor to the cause he professed to serve. Companions in crime, they were destined to share the same chastisement. The Duke of Maddaloni, in accordance with the Viceroy's instructions, repaired on horseback to the market-place. There he sought by gracious language and lavish promises of freedom from taxation in the future and pardon for offences in the past, to tranquillize the people. A chorus of voices replied, "We will never hold our peace till we have in our possession the original of the Charter granted by the Emperor Charles V."

* Nicolai, "Historia del ultime Rivolutioni di Napoli, p. 42. Capecelatro, "Diario," p. 34.

The aristocratic envoy, though encircled by a guard of nobles, was dismayed by the menacing uproar around him, and withdrew in haste, promising to return with the original document. Thus ended the first attempt at negotiation on the part of Don Diomed Carafa.

CHAPTER VII.

The intellect of Italy at the period of the rebellion of the year 1647 was brilliantly represented by the followers of pictorial art. The name of Salvator Rosa is associated as painter and patriot with a twofold and eternal fame. His genius, like that of many of the Italian painters, especially those of the Neapolitan school, was elevated by a rare and lofty spirit of independence surpassing that shown by the majority of the statesmen or warriors of the time. The intellectual and patriotic aspirations of Italy shone resplendent in the glorious achievements of their hands and the heroic efforts of their lives.

It is not surprising that, sympathizing with the spirit of reform, impatient for progress and intolerant of abuse, the members of the Neapolitan school of painters should have joined the insurrection under Masaniello, ennobling it by their co-operation and the association of their illustrious names.

But a private motive also was influential in the formation of the secret and indomitable corps known as the *Compagnia della Morte.*

A kinsman of Aniello Falcone, the painter, having been killed during the open day in an altercation with some Spanish soldiers, Aniello, rallying his pupils round him, had attacked the soldiers in return. During this affray one of the company of painters was killed, and the rest were compelled to fly, while the Spanish soldiers were shielded from all fear of chastisement through the protection afforded them by the government. In consequence of these events, the followers of Aniello, summoning their relations and friends, provided themselves with arms, elected their master for their leader, and took an oath of vengeance against their Spanish foes.

The two Francazanos, scholars of Spagnoletto, Viviano Codagora, Andrea Vaccaro, a follower of Guido Rene, Carlo Coppola, Micco Spadaro, whose graphic representations record the stirring events of his time, and Salvator Rosa, who exhibited in his paintings the bold unshrinking spirit which characterized him as a man, joined the Death Company.

Hardship, adventure, and heroic exploit, seem to have been the inheritance of the Neapolitan school of painters. The life of Salvator Rosa in itself was a romance from his earliest years, when, thrashed by the Carmelite monks for indulging his genius by drawing with charcoal on the white walls of their convent, to the period, marked by wandering and vicissitudes, of his later life, when, armed with sword and dagger, he marched as a member of the Death Company, and finally had to fly for refuge with Falcone, whose pupil he had been, to Rome.

In order to carry out the principles of the Society, those who had joined it gladly incurred sacrifices of every kind, and with noble self-denial supported themselves by painting during the night, in consequence of which Carlo Coppola is said to have lost his sight.

Aniello Falcone was a distinguished master of the Neapolitan school. The salient characteristic of his daring genius is shown in the delineation of battles, in which his intimate knowledge of military matters is always conspicuous.

Domenico Garguili, called Micco Spadaro,

possessed an extraordinary talent for painting miniature figures, which he introduced with such infinite grace that Viviano Codagora would not permit other artists to add the figures in his pieces. This circumstance led to an intimate friendship which lasted between the two artists till the moment when they risked their lives in the same cause. Micco Spadaro had perhaps no equal in depicting the manners and costumes of the working classes of his own country, and in some of his pieces representing large assemblies, the number of figures introduced is found to have exceeded a thousand. Micco Spadaro, like Salvator Rosa, frequently portrayed the fisherman of Amalfi, and, in one remarkable painting of Spadaro's, Masaniello is depicted richly attired, wearing a dress of silver brocade, with a plumed hat, and a gorgeously decorated sword. A medallion, representing the Madonna of Carmel, is displayed upon his breast. Thus magnificently equipped, and riding a white horse, he leads on a boisterous throng.

The intrepid Company speedily proffered its services to Masaniello. The ardour of its members for the revolutionary cause incited still more the hatred of the Spaniards, though, for awhile, this disaffection on the side of the painters was overlooked, mainly through a fear on the part of the Spaniards of molesting those who stood well with the populace, and in a less degree through the influence exerted on their behalf by the luxurious and ill-fated Giuseppe Ribera, surnamed Lo Spagnoletto, who, although a teacher of the revolutionist, Francazano, was greatly in favour with the viceroyal party.

Masaniello not only accepted the active services of the Company of Death, but was accustomed to hold counsel with its members in the solitary Tower of the Carmelites, a sombre spot adjoining the convent which had been formerly used by the monks for purposes of religious punishment. This gloomy retreat, with its bare walls and rough benches but scantily lighted, in which self-tortured Asceticism once performed its expiatory service, now constituted an altar where were offered the vows of a different worship. Here at nightfall the chosen confederates assembled, as did the clubs of the Jacobins and Cordeliers in the old convents of France, at a later hour of a mightier Revolution. The noblest intellect and the most heroic virtue in the land of Italy were dedicated to the service of liberty, when it numbered amongst its disciples Salvator Rosa and Masaniello. Genius and patriotism were stirred by the agitation of the time to a sublime enthusiasm and eloquence, and the heart of the entire nation was kindled in irresistible response.

CHAPTER VIII.

The dawn of the 9th of July broke amidst fresh scenes of disorder and desolation. Numbers continued to swell the torrent of revolution, which threatened to overwhelm with fire and sword everything in its course. Flames arose in all quarters of Naples, as though the lovely city were about to be consumed by conflagration. Those noble Neapolitan palaces, the magnificence of which has never been surpassed, fell in blackened fragments to the earth, while their superb contents, the treasured fruits of avarice or the proud boast of ambition, were scattered and destroyed. The splendour of these possessions affords an insight into the luxuries enjoyed by the aristocracy of the time. Such, indeed, was the mania for magnificent display, that a special decree was issued by the Duke of Ossuna, to prohibit the employment of gilders in private houses until a certain galleon, then in course of construction, had been completed.* The silver and gold with which the wealthy thus decorated their habitations was as lavishly displayed in their furniture and on their tables. The velvet and silken carpets in use were almost invariably interwoven with gold, or of a still more costly texture, exquisitely wrought, acquired the classic name of Arazzi. Those proud creations which the unequalled art of the age had given to the world, fashioned from marble, bronze, glass, and the precious metals, into forms of infinite variety and unrivalled grace, glittered abundantly in the palaces of the nobles. But all such treasures were relentlessly destroyed by the insurgents, while the affrighted owners looked on from the forts and watch-towers to which they had fled. The tumult of martial music and the roar of artillery filled the city. Revolution reigned, and the great Nemesis was revealed amidst the horrors of anarchy and disaster.

The nobility, who felt their lives no less than property to be in danger, fled on all sides. Don Carlo Capecelatro, warned of the danger which threatened him from having constantly defended the privileges of the nobility against the rights of

* Zazzera, "Governo del Duca d'Ossuna."

the people, took care at once to place his wife and child in safety. Then he went alone to Giovanni Battista di Franco, Marquis of Postiglione, to ask him for secret shelter for one night, until he could find security elsewhere. But the terror of these tumultuous times had snapped asunder the closest ties. Giovanni Battista, the intimate friend of Capecelatro, who had rendered him service in his direst need, now panic-stricken, demurred about receiving his old friend. At two o'clock in the morning, before Don Capecelatro was asleep, news was brought that a great crowd had assembled at the house of the noble Prince of Colle, who dwelt with his brother Francesco di Somma. Already the fire was kindled in the square before their abode. At this intelligence Capecelatro, perceiving the increasing terror of his host, who now lamented aloud, dressed and went forth at once, heedless of peril. Traversing a part of the city lit up by the lurid fires of revolution, he passed on to Pizzofalcone, where he was warmly received at the house of a friend, less pusillanimous than the Marquis. Thence, two days afterwards, Don Capecelatro passed to Castel Nuovo, where he remained until the close of the Revolution.*

* Capecelatro, "Diario," p. 51.

Meanwhile Francesco di Somma and the Prince of Colle thus closely pressed, taking their families with them, retreated to an adjacent church to find a sanctuary. But Francesco barely escaped with his life. The populace, on arriving at the court-yard of his house, found the entrance defended only by a single faithful domestic. The remainder, a considerable number, had taken to flight. Francesco di Somma, sword in hand, stationed himself in a winding staircase, determined to defend himself to his last breath. The insurgents, having entered, sought him with shouts and menaces. Francesco, as he encountered them, asked "why they wished to assail him?" They answered by tearing a valuable ring off his finger. This they threw, with some costly household ornaments, into the flames that blazed in the square. Whilst Francesco was in this dilemma, a party sent by Don Tommaso Caracciolo, came to his aid and assisted him in making his retreat to the church.*

Those who despised the warnings of the times had reason to repent their false confidence. The Duke of Caivano, when counselled to take care of his property, replied contemptuously,

* Capecelatro, "Diario," p. 51.

"*non ho paura di quattro scalzi;*"* yet these "paltry vagabonds" brought terror and destruction to his hearth. The Duke of Caivano was Secretary-General of State, and had made himself hated by the people through using his high official influence to their disadvantage. The costly contents of the Duke's palace at Santa Chiara, a magnificent library of great value and the documents of chancery under his care, the destruction of which was regarded as an irreparable loss to the State, were alike sacrificed by the revolutionists.† Still they continued to call for vengeance, and to urge upon Masaniello the necessity of punishing the oppressors of the people. A list was drawn up, containing the names of thirty-six persons whose houses they intended to burn.‡ The offences alleged against them were the farming of tolls and the imposition of inordinate taxes. In this way they had been enriched at the expense of the people. Ministers, aristocrats, and traders alike, by these nefarious practices, had preyed upon the wretched Neapolitans. According to a proverb of the time, the Spanish ministers

* De Santis, "Historia di Napoli," p. 51.

† Baldacchini, "Storia Napoletana," p. 58.

‡ Capecelatro, "Diario," p. 27.

"gnawed in Sicily, but devoured in Naples." "Let us go and burn up the wealth of these traitors who have taken our life's blood," cried the insurgents as they rushed to destroy the magnificent abode of Cesare Lubrano, a government contractor. The contents of his palace were not found so costly as it was anticipated, which instantly gave rise to the idea that the property had been concealed in the monastery close by. Thither the revolutionists repaired, and demanded the surrender of whatever was hidden. The monks denied and opposed in vain. "Bring the riches forth," exclaimed the assailants, "or you will soon see your sacred edifice on fire." This, as the monks well knew, was no idle threat, and sufficed to make them yield without further question the costly accumulations concealed.*

At the sack of the dwelling of Andrea Mazzola, another government contractor, the people acquired a fresh and ample supply of arms. Mazzola was one of those Genoese traders who were held in such detestation by the Neapolitans. He had recently imported a large quantity of arms from Genoa for the use of the royal troops, but desirous of payment before relinquishing them, had

* De Santis, "Historia di Napoli," p. 73.

retained them in his possession. They were seized at once as a glorious booty by the people, who informed their owner that he need not disturb himself about the matter, for when the weapons were no longer needed in the service of the revolt, that they should then be returned. Mazzola dared to answer by a menace of chastisement, when the insurgents, not content with the arms they had acquired, destroyed the entire contents of his habitation.

In the midst of these disorders the revolutionists still maintained their war-cry of "Long life to the King; down with the bad government."* They lauded the memory of the Emperor Charles V., and to show their reverence for the reigning monarch, carried his portrait with that of the Emperor in a procession, under richly-decorated canopies, through the streets.† These portraits, as well as those of religious subjects, were carefully kept from destruction, and wherever they were exhibited the place was free from assault. Thus the insurgents desired to express their willingness to obey legitimate authority, and

* Antonio de Tarsia, "Tumultos de la Ciudad de Napoles," p. 59.

† Donzelli, "Partenope Liberata," p. 55.

their right to protest against its maladministration. When the Cardinal Filomarino declared, on the part of the Viceroy, a pardon for the rebels, a fresh disturbance arose. "They had no need," said the revolutionists, "of pardon, for they were not rebels. They preserved unbroken faith to the King, and they wished only for a right administration of the laws."*

Cardinal Filomarino endeavoured, with the utmost zeal, to mitigate the disorders.† He exhorted the people with the warmest prayers, nor were his benevolent efforts altogether unavailing.

Other mediators were scarcely less actively employed. Montesarchio, accompanied by six nobles, proceeded to the market-place on a deputation of peace. The treatment he and his friends received convinced them of the grave peril which would in future attach to such embassies. The Neapolitans judged truly that all these negotiations were but to give time to their adversaries to mature preparations for their chastisement.‡ Their distrust was heightened by the continual substitution of new documents for the original

* Botta, "Storia d'Italia," vol. vi. p. 323.

† Tontoli, "Il Masaniello," p. 60.

‡ Ibid.

charter. The cry arose more tumultuously than ever, "To arms, to arms."

Montesarchio, the leader of the deputation to the market-place, was seized by the hair, and thus dragged from the saddle. The six nobles who attended him were retained in captivity.*

Notwithstanding these proceedings, the Duke of Maddaloni, with the reckless daring which characterized him, repaired again to the market, but soon had reason to repent his temerity. He was received with shouts and terrible execrations. All his efforts at conciliation, his promises and protestations, were lost in the clamour and confusion around him. "Treachery, treachery!" was echoed on every side, whilst the crowd, pressing closely round the Duke, succeeded in dragging him off his horse.† Masaniello himself, incensed at the perfidious declarations of the Duke, was foremost in the assault.‡ With jeers and blows he returned the outrages which he had suffered at the hands of the Duke's underlings, who had robbed the poor fisherman by taking his merchandise without payment.§

* Capecelatro, "Diario," p. 38.

† Baldacchini, "Storia Napoletana," p. 55.

‡ De Santis, "Historia di Napoli," p. 62.

§ Capecelatro, "Diario."

The Duke of Maddaloni was then closely bound, and handed over with ignominy as a prisoner to Beradino Grasso and Perrone.

The fact of Masaniello having surrendered the Duke into the especial custody of these two men, proves the entire confidence he placed in them. Little did the unfortunate Masaniello dream of the good fellowship and strict alliance which existed between these base colleagues and his sworn enemy, the Duke of Maddaloni.

The Viceroy meantime, anxious for the safety of the Duke, had sent the prior of the Johannites, Gregorio Carafa, who was brother of the Prince of Roccella, and afterwards made Grand Master of Malta, to endeavour to persuade the people to release the envoys. The Prior, although a Carafa, was a man of amiable qualities. He addressed the people in the most conciliatory language; and presented to them a fresh declaration of rights, in substance the same as the one offered to them by the Duke. But the Prior also was received with derision and upbraided, and stigmatized as an impostor. The populace now broke into fierce menaces. "All the nobles of the city are clearly our enemies," they cried.

There were no longer bounds to the popular desire for the destruction of the aristocracy. The

Prior indeed was glad to escape with his life, and retreated in haste under the plea of seeking the original charter which the people had incessantly demanded, and which they desired that the Viceroy, the Collateral Council, and the Council of State should, by a Public Act, be compelled to observe. A report was spread that the charter could not be found, for the farmers of the tolls were strangely averse to giving it into the hands of the people.

Whilst a pretence of pacific measures was still made by the Viceroy, the utmost circumspection was exercised by the government in taking military precautions. Orders were given for the reinforcement of the arsenals and fortresses. The heights of Pizzofalcone and other available points were carefully guarded.* Care was taken to defend especially the quarter of the Court, and the greater number of troops were accordingly stationed there. The Viceregal forces, consisting of Spaniards, Italians, and Germans, were formed into divisions, and placed at convenient points. A squadron in the square of the palace kept the Pizzofalcone quarter. The new bridge of the Mortelle was fortified. The streets

* Nicolai, "Historia del ultime Rivolutioni di Napoli," p. 45.

communicating with the shore of the sea of Santa Lucia were enclosed, and barricades were everywhere erected of barrels of earth, sacks of wool, and faggots, and when these failed, the boughs of the magnificent fruit trees of the royal park. A gate of the Castel Nuovo, communicating with a bridge in the park, alone was left unfortified, but the bridge was kept raised, and the place was diligently watched by Field-Marshal Tuttavilla.*

With the exception of the Pizzofalcone quarter, the Royal Palace, and the castles Nuovo and St Elmo, Naples was in the hands of the insurgents. The fortresses of St Elmo and Nuovo were so deficient in ammunition and provisions,† that a few days would have sufficed for their surrender had the revolutionists pressed the siege.

But at this juncture an event occurred, not less decisive in its influence on the Revolution than in the fortunes of its leader. This was a public announcement that the original charter, containing the rights and immunities conceded to the city by the Emperor Charles, had at length

* Capecelatro, "Diario," pp. 46, 47.

† Documenti degli Agenti del Gran Duca di Toscana. Archivio Storico, vol. ix.

been discovered.* It was entrusted by the Viceroy to the Cardinal Filomarino, who lost no time in repairing with it to the market-place.†

A sincere dèsire for peace was in the heart of Masaniello. Not until repeated remonstrance, expostulation, and entreaty on the part of the nation had failed, did he resort to open defiance. No sanguinary excesses had as yet marked the course of the insurrection. The Revolution had preserved itself hitherto unstained by the worst license of civil war; and even the hostilities and destruction of property which it involved had been characterized by noble instances of temperance and magnanimity.

Masaniello, by issuing the most stringent decrees, sought to uphold a lofty spirit on the part of the people. Urged by the irresistible impetuosity of his adherents, he had consented that the list should be drawn out of the incendiaries they intended to commit, not at his instigation, although with the sanction which he was scarcely in a position to withhold. His sole desire now was to suppress disorders, and to ensure a peaceful realization of the reforms for which he had so

* Capecelatro, "Diario," p. 48.

† Baldacchini, "Storia Napoletana," p. 64.

ardently toiled, by a public act which should bind the viceregal government under solemn oath to the observance of the Imperial Charter. In accordance with these motives, Masaniello now desisted from further aggressive measures, or there is little doubt that the troops who were conquerors at St Lorenzo would have made themselves masters of the remaining strongholds of the city.*

As a first step towards a cessation of warfare, Masaniello caused the people to assemble in the market-place, in order to explain to them the conditions upon which he sought an inauguration of peace. At the same time it was agreed that an interview should take place between Masaniello and the Viceroy at the palace, which was to be followed by a celebration of the peace in the Carmelite Cathedral, when the Viceroy, in the presence of the dignitaries of the realm and of the leaders of the Revolution, should bind himself by oath to the observance of the charter.

The scene at the market-place at this juncture was one of intense excitement. The Neapolitans felt that a momentous epoch had arrived. The

* This is admitted by the impartial testimony of Capecelatro, who was animated by little democratic sympathy.

present crisis would decide whether the bitter bondage of centuries should cease or be riveted with stronger fetters. Outrage, oppression, and slavery constituted the black retrospect their memory invoked. They panted for release from the hateful and dreaded yoke under which they had groaned, but the thought of freedom appeared too sweet to be other than an illusion. They reflected on the traditional perfidy of the Spaniards, and were filled with distrust. One hope, one desire, animated the vast multitude. Separating into groups, they talked earnestly and eagerly amongst themselves concerning the pending negotiations. Clamour and violence were suppressed, and the fiercest passions were stilled, now that the boon desired for centuries seemed within their grasp. How best to ensure peace—the lasting Peace which is the golden fruit of Liberty alone? This question of absorbing interest was on every tongue. Some of the citizens, more enlightened or less sanguine than their fellows, were agitated by strange forebodings.

The assembly with one accord demanded the charter, which they wished to have in their own hands in order to prove its completeness and authenticity. They desired also that the articles of capitulation should be drawn up by one of their own party. The conveyancing of the terms of the treaty and the investigation of the charter were entrusted, therefore, to Genuino,* upon whose matured judgment—for he was now eighty years of age—sagacity, and experience, the populace relied. The wily adventurer, unhappily, possessed the entire confidence of Masaniello, who was accustomed to depend unquestioningly upon his counsel. The seeming patriot would gladly have crushed the Revolution at this crisis. Seeking only his own interests, he wished, like too many other leaders of popular movements, to arrest the insurrection at the point most convenient to himself. Hitherto, he had been allured by the promise of the Viceroy to create him President of the Royal Chamber, and he now exerted his influence to obtain the promotion of Francesco Arpaia, who had been his companion in his wanderings and an accomplice in his crimes. His machinations were successful, and Arpaia was publicly proclaimed Deputy of the people, in place of Naclerio.

The night of the 9th was passed in hot discussion between Masaniello and a chosen number

* Donzelli, "Partenope Liberata," p. 27. Baldacchini, "Storia Napoletana," p. 63.

of his adherents respecting the terms of the treaty. Their meeting was held in the Convent of the Carmelites, where the indefatigable Cardinal Filomarino was also in attendance. So unremitting were the efforts of the Cardinal to ensure the fulfilment of the treaty, that his time was occupied night and day in facilitating the requisite negotiations. Exhorting in the cathedral or giving counsel in the convent, his energy and enthusiasm continued unabated.

The approval by Genuino of the charter was hailed with universal joy as the advent of Peace.

CHAPTER IX.

After the conquest of St Lorenzo on the 9th, Masaniello received triumphal honours in the city.* He was now virtually sovereign of Naples. Soul of the Revolution, his decisions had undisputed sway.† The acknowledged chief of more than a hundred thousand followers, who were devoted in their adherence to him, the destiny of the city was in his hands.‡ In a few days this remarkable man had attained to a marvellous height of power, and exercised a command which kept an entire people in subjection. He had, indeed, become a king in the city, and one who proved himself the most glorious and triumphant

* Baldacchini, "Storia Napoletana," p. 63.

† Giannone, "Storia di Napoli."

‡ Documenti degli Agenti del Gran Duca di Toscana. Archivio Storico Italiano, vol. ix.

in the world.* "It would truly be impossible so to magnify his authority," writes one quaint chronicler of the Revolution, "but that much more would remain to be said." Never, perhaps, in the history of nations had the absolute government of a city such as Naples been held by a ruler of so humble an origin. Yet the people were blind in their subjection. It was rather adoration than reverence which Masaniello received, and a gesture from him was sufficient to sway the multitude, who had implicit faith in their leader.† Such is the unanimous testimony of contemporary writers with respect to the chief of the Neapolitan Revolution.

Success not unfrequently brings to light characteristics utterly at variance with those which have hitherto been manifested by the same individual. The imperial masters of Rome sometimes appeared amiable until they assumed the Purple.

What was the effect of prosperity on the character of Masaniello? During the period of revolutionary triumph he continued to show justice, prudence, and moderation.‡ He resolutely

* Lettere del Cardinal Filomarino.

‡ Tontoli, "Il Masaniello," p. 48.

‡ Lettere del Cardinal Filomarino. Archivio Storico Italiano.

refused all offers of emolument and aggrandizement; nor would he assume a single title of command, save that of Captain-General of the People.* Retaining the dress and mode of living suited to the original humility of his position,† neither conquests, honours, nor homage, caused him to swerve in the least from the noble simplicity of his nature. Clad in his mariner's dress of white linen, leaving the breast bared, as represented in so many portraits of the Fisherman of Naples, Masaniello was accustomed to give audience on a rude platform, erected near his dwelling.‡ That strange tribunal constituted his only throne, and there, holding a sword, which had the power of a sceptre, Masaniello gave laws or forbade measures, as he thought expedient. He was at once the leader, judge, and counsellor of the Neapolitans, by whom he was obeyed with unquestioning submission. Now issuing decrees, now marching at the head of his forces, Masaniello was the centre and the source of power. Even the least enthusiastic narrators of the insurrection do not deny their high admiration to

* Tontoli, "Il Masaniello," pp. 94, 95.

† Baldacchini, "Storia Napoletana," p. 68.

‡ Antonio di Tarsia, "Tumultos de la Ciudad de Napoles," p. 97.

the poor fisherman who, through a strange vicissitude of fortune, was destined to play so heroic a part in the history of his country. The aspiration of his life had been to secure to the Neapolitans the boon desired by them for centuries. This was the restitution of those rights which had been accorded by the Emperor Charles V. To this object the thoughts, the energies, and the hopes of Masaniello had been continually directed. The insolent pride of the nobles, which had been the bane of the poor, the insurrection had, for a time at least, effectually checked. Henceforth their arbitrary power Masaniello fondly hoped would be held in subjection by the reform which introduced an equalization of votes, through which the voice of the people would in future be heard in all matters important to their interests.

Masaniello improved by his excellent judgment the triumph his valour had won. He showed superior wisdom in the transaction of civil and military affairs. Veteran soldiers were astonished at the knowledge displayed in the propriety of his martial operations,* and Ducal envoys gave their highest testimony to the admirable measures

* Botta, "Storia d' Italia," vol. vi. p. 326.

of his government.* Compared with the triumph of reformers in any age, the achievements of Masaniello during the transitory period of his rule were no insignificant accomplishments. Like Rienzi, who, through the force of his judicious and vigorous decrees, remodelled the polity of Rome, Masaniello changed the entire aspect of the Neapolitan State, which was rapidly transformed under his rule. Masaniello, holding councils, issuing decrees, directing operations, and in perpetual activity to secure the realization of his cherished plans, denied himself sleep and refreshment; and was accustomed to assemble in conference with his chosen friends during the night, in order to modify, consolidate, or amplify the code of administration drawn up. He was absorbed in redressing the wrongs of the people, and in devoting himself to their welfare.

Every precaution was accordingly taken for the security of the city and its environs. A declaration was published by Masaniello prohibiting further incendiaries under penalty of death. The same edict ordered the inhabitants of Naples to remain quietly in their dwellings, forbade the

* Documenti degli Agenti del Gran Duca di Toscana. Archivio Storico Italiano.

molestation of traders or vendors of any kind of provisions, commanded the militia to refrain from attacking the foreign soldiery, and bound them to remain fully equipped and prepared for action at the posts assigned to them. A prohibition was issued also against the sale of provisions at a higher price than they had commanded previously to the recent imposition of taxes.*

Tranquillity appeared to descend once more on the agitated city, and the Neapolitans were glad at heart in the near prospect of a settled peace.

This crisis of the Revolution was the turning point—irrevocable in its influence for good or ill upon the history of the Revolution, and upon the career of its originator. Abundant evidence proves that Masaniello diligently improved the brief period of his rule to advance the welfare of the community. Unhappily an exaggerated confidence on the part of Masaniello in those who least deserved his trust, blighted all hopes of permanent benefit from the Revolution, and sacrificed the welfare of the unfortunate man who had devoted his best energies to the cause.

* Nicolai, "Historia del ultime Rivolutioni di Napoli," p. 49. Tontoli, "Il Masaniello," p. 46.

The morning of the 10th of July broke amidst the content and rejoicing of the nation. A momentous innovation, often a work of years, had, as it were, been effected in a single day. Conservatism, which had been dominant through centuries, had in a sharp and sudden conflict been overcome by the principle of change. National enthusiasm had served the cause of wisdom, and from out the suffering, sacrifice, and turmoil under which generations had groaned, a new political life appeared to have arisen for the Neapolitans. They awaited in breathless expectation the solemn inauguration of peace about to take place in the Cathedral of the Carmelites.

Masaniello had convoked an assembly of the militia with their respective captains, and the counsellors of the people were commanded also to be in attendance at the market-place. Here in conference they awaited the ceremonial in the Cathedral. The neighbourhood of the church and the convent was thronged with a multitude eager to learn the result of the treaty. The Cathedral itself was densely crowded. Cardinal Filomarino with Masaniello were in attendance there, and the ceremony was about to commence, when a troop of five hundred men, armed and mounted, were seen to approach the market-place.*

The banditti, then as now the pest of the Italian soil, were the chosen agents of the feudal lords, who found in them a ready means of perpetrating acts of ruffianism.

The Duke of Maddaloni, enraged at the treatment he had received from Masaniello at the market-place, had resolved that the same spot, already replete with tragic memories, should be the scene of a dire revenge.† The plot which he had conceived was willingly seconded by his supposed jailor—a man capable of every atrocity, and who saw with envy the increasing greatness of Masaniello.‡ The Duke of Maddaloni, through the connivance of this traitor, had regained his liberty ere the close of the very day on which he had been made captive. The night was spent in diligently organizing the conspiracy which he hoped would ensure the downfall of Masaniello.

The ferocious retainers of the Duke had divided into small companies, and had contrived thus to enter at intervals under various pretexts

* Donzelli, "Partenope Liberata," p. 31. De Santis, "Historia di Napoli," p. 89.

† Baldacchini, "Storia Napoletana," p. 73.

‡ De Santis, "Historia di Napoli," p. 89.

within the precincts of the city. Part on horse and part on foot, they were quartered at different points along the main streets in the direction of the market. Then gradually closing in a body, they advanced towards the given spot at the moment settled for action.

By this arrangement the conspirators hoped to succeed in scattering the people through the suddenness of the assault, and by firing upon them mercilessly, should they, after the destruction of Masaniello in the cathedral, turn in vengeance on his assassins.* The multitude suddenly amazed, and without the presence of their leader, would, they imagined, be speedily dispersed or exterminated.

It is said that Perrone was within the Cathedral, and under pretence of having important intelligence to communicate to Masaniello, glided to the side of his unsuspecting companion.† Immediately the signal was given to those without by some of the bandits who had entered the church. A shot was fired by one of them at Masaniello, who hastening to the portals, cried

* Donzelli, "Partenope Liberata," p. 31.

† De Santis, "Historia di Napoli," p. 89. Antonio de Tarsia, "Tumultos de la Ciudad de Napoles," p. 66.

"Treason."* Again a shot was fired, and another and another successively were aimed at the leader of the people by the traitors, not one of which, however, succeeded in wounding Masaniello,† though he was unarmed, and wore his usual simple attire. This extraordinary escape convinced the Neapolitans that a special interposition had been effected on his behalf by the gracious Lady of Carmel.

At the cry of Masaniello his adherents rushed impetuously into the church.‡ With shouts and cries they called furiously for vengeance on the base hirelings who had menaced the life of Masaniello. The design had failed. The conspirators were defeated, and they saw that they had miscalculated the strength of a people nerved to superior power in a righteous cause. Masaniello, so dear to the hearts of his followers, still lived to defy the intrigues of his numerous enemies, and his devoted adherents were animated by fresh courage at the thought.

A frightful tumult ensued. The sacred altar itself was turned into a scene of slaughter. In

* Donzelli, "Partenope Liberata," p. 32.

† Capecelatro, "Diario," p. 53.

‡ Baldacchini, "Storia Napoletana," p. 74.

vain the conspirators sought concealment in the cells, cloisters, and dormitories of the adjacent convent. The fury of the people followed them, and followed them relentlessly, everywhere. At the High Altar itself and in the sacristy they were slain. Within the churches and without the work of blood went on, leaving the dead and wounded in all directions.* The brother of Perrone, and Perrone himself, were among those who sought a sanctuary in the convent.† There they took refuge in a cell which they fruitlessly attempted to barricade against their pursuers. The door was opened, and Perrone, who in the close prospect of his inevitable doom, had thrown himself on his knees entreating one of the monks to guard him and give him absolution, was confronted by his implacable assailants.‡ Torn from the protection of the monk, he was killed on the spot. In vain he had protested his innocence. It did not avert the violent doom which he had long since merited by his crimes, and now met with from the very men who but a few days before had given him their entire trust and alle-

* Baldacchini, "Storia Napoletana," p. 75.

†De Santis, "Historia di Napoli," p. 90.

‡ Donzelli, "Partenope Liberata," p. 32.

giance. The monk who had endeavoured to shield him was reviled by the infuriated people as a protector of traitors, and, trembling with fear whilst he pressed the figure of the Virgin to his breast, he supplicated for mercy, declaring that simple charity alone had prompted him to shelter Perrone, and that he was in utter ignorance of the affair. He was then left unmolested.

The brother of Perrone had concealed himself under a bed in one of the dormitories, but seeing that he was on the point of discovery, hastened to a high window, and, in desperation, took one terrific leap into the court-yard below.*

There were no bounds to the tumult which prevailed. All again was anarchy, for perfidy had brought a bitter blight upon the fair promise of peace, greeted with so much joy by the Neapolitans. The people now hurried to and fro infuriated, and menacing with cries of "Slaughter, slaughter."†

Cardinal Filomarino meanwhile had repaired to the private room of the Superior of the Convent. There he was in imminent peril of his life. Sincere and zealous in his endeavours to obtain

* De Santis, "Historia di Napoli," p. 90.

† Baldacchini, "Storia Napoletana," p. 76.

peace, he was dauntless in confronting the perils of warfare, and forgetful of all risk when labouring for the good of the community. Many persons, looking for safety in his presence, followed him into the apartment of the Superior. One man, inadvertently opening the casement, received a deadly wound from one of the multitude without, who mistook him for a bandit.* A succession of shots were fired into the room. Whilst the wounded man lay bleeding at the feet of the Cardinal the assailants proceeded to storm the chamber, when Filomarino, with characteristic intrepidity, prevented further conflict by opening the door.

The crowd without assured him that they had come only in search of traitors.† They then bitterly lamented that treachery should have put an end to their hopes of consummating the peace.‡ The Cardinal endeavoured by every possible argument to moderate their transport of anger.

Whilst a portion of the infuriated multitude had hastened to storm the apartment in which the Cardinal had taken refuge, another detach-

* Capecelatri, "Diario," p. 54.

† Donzelli, "Partenope Liberata," p. 33.

‡ Baldacchini, "Storia Napoletana," p. 76.

ment was in pursuit of Antino Grasso, who, from having been the confidant and ally of Perrone, was suspected, and not without cause, by the people. Grasso, like his companions in arms, Perrone and Genuino, was a mercenary, who had passed through various adventures in the several countries where he had served as a soldier. His restless career had been spent in embroilments and feuds, and his unquiet spirit had eagerly taken part in the Revolution.* Professedly its enthusiastic adherent, he was in reality an ally of the Viceroy. Under the mask of facilitating the negotiations for peace, he had sought frequent interviews with the Cardinal Filomarino, whom it is supposed he was commissioned to assassinate.† He was, moreover, an active agent of the conspiracy organized by the Duke of Maddaloni, for which he now paid a bitter penalty, as, pierced by many wounds, he sought protection from the very man whom it is said he purposed to destroy. Prostrate at the feet of the Cardinal, he embraced his knees, and implored mercy.‡ He entreated that the last fatal stroke might be

* Donzelli, "Partenope Liberata," p. 34.

† Capecelatro, "Diario," p. 55.

‡ Baldacchini, "Storia Napoletana," p. 76. De Santis, "Historia di Napoli," p. 91.

for a brief space at least averted, in order, he said, to allow him time to reveal a frightful conspiracy which he knew was in operation for the destruction of the people.* He then disclosed the design of the brothers Maddaloni to destroy a considerable portion of the city, including the cathedral and monastery of the Carmelites and the adjacent quarter of the market. The artillery had been, he affirmed, already laid, and the Neapolitan Nero only awaited the close of evening, when the spot would be most abundantly thronged, to put his design in execution. Other troops of bandits would then be in attendance, and speedily complete the work of destruction by the slaughter of those whom the conflagration chanced to spare.

Whether the Duke of Maddaloni and his brother, base as they undeniably were, had in reality entertained so atrocious a scheme, appears doubtful. It is asserted, however, that some monks discovered sundry barrels of powder under the foundation of the monastery, which aided in confirming the supposition of the plot having been actually conceived. If it were sim-

* Antonio de Tarsia, "Tumultos de la Ciudad de Napoles," p. 66.

ply an invention of Grasso to avert his doom, the expedient failed, for the people, now convinced of his treachery, speedily inflicted the last mortal stroke. The people, in the infatuation of unbounded wrath, expressed their abhorrence of their foes by unseemly acts of irreverence towards their remains, which were dragged through the streets and left without burial.* The heads of the traitors were carried on pikes through the city. The people, in this first ungovernable impulse of their fury, no longer shrank from excesses which as yet had not dishonoured their cause.

A rumour spread that some bandits were sheltered in the church of the Capuchins. A detachment of the insurgents accordingly surrounded the place, and succeeded in chasing them out of the sanctuary. Seven of the number were killed.† Now, indeed, commenced that crusade against the banditti which was carried on until the close of the Revolution. During the panic that prevailed immediately subsequent to the Maddaloni conspiracy, all those known or suspected to be bandits were captured or killed

* "Diario" di Capecelatro, p. 54.

† Donzelli, "Partenope Liberata," p. 55.

by the troops of Masaniello. Those who had signalized themselves in securing them were rewarded by the popular chief with military promotion.*

The national hatred of the Duke of Maddaloni had by this time increased tenfold. The Duke, after his liberation by his jailor Perrone, had fled in disguise, and reached unrecognized the heights of Capo di Monte. Thence he wandered to Chiazano, and at this point met with an acquaintance on horse-back, who lent him his horse. Through the aid thus afforded him he managed to reach Cardito, where he found temporary shelter.

Armed masses meantime fled in different directions to seek the Duke. A report having arisen that he was in the village of Arenella, a crowd ran thither in pursuit. Two of the Duke's servants were captured, but the unfortunate men, though cruelly pressed to declare where their master was, either through fidelity or ignorance, did not reveal. They were accordingly conducted to the head-quarters of Masaniello, who showed his good sense and benevolence by allowing them to depart in peace.†

* Capecelatro, "Diario," p. 55.

† Baldacchini, "Storia Napoletana," p. 86.

The people, unsuccessful in their endeavours to capture the Duke a second time, now exerted their efforts in search of Don Giuseppe, his brother. A Carafa, at all events, should suffer, in order that his fate might prove a terrible example of justice. It was discovered that Don Giuseppe, with the Prior of Roccella and several followers, had taken refuge in the convent of Santa Maria la Nuova.* Upon a height inclining precipitately to the harbour, its descent covered with steep, damp little streets containing some miserable habitations, stands the great Franciscan convent. There, in all probability, Don Giuseppe had awaited the wished-for intelligence of success in the attempt on the life of Masaniello. Thither Masaniello sent a company of more than four hundred men with orders to lay siege to the convent, and to seize the fugitives.† Don Giuseppe was hidden in the most obscure part of the building. He wished to inform the Viceroy of his perilous position, and to entreat him to open fire on the assailants in order to disperse them and facilitate his escape.‡

* De Santis, "Historia di Napoli," p. 93.

† Capecelatro, "Diario," p. 56.

‡ Donzelli, "Partenope Liberata," p. 36.

Accordingly he entrusted a note to a monk, who, concealing it in his cowl, thought thus to reach Castel Nuovo in safety. But the bearer was interrupted in his course, the note discovered, and the poor monk paid the penalty of his share in the transaction by receiving a grievous wound.* The gates of the monastery, which had been closed, were fired by the people. With shouts demanding their foes, they rushed in. Soon the courts and corridors were filled with the furious conquerors, but the dark cloisters and irregular windings of the old conventual edifice baffled their pursuit. A domestic of the household of Carafa, wandering terror-stricken through the dim corridors, was encountered and killed.

Don Giuseppe, who well knew the danger of his position, hastily assumed the garb of the Capuchin monks, and descended through secret passages to the back of the building. Thence he, with the Prior of Roccella, escaped into the dark narrow street of the soap manufacturers (*Saponari*). At this point the fugitives separated, in order the better to avoid detection. The Prior passing boldly on, at length took refuge,† when

* Capecelatro, "Diario," p. 56.

† Donzelli, "Partenope Liberata," p. 57.

exhausted, in the house of a dyer, who was too honest to betray him, and afterwards made his way during the night to Castel Nuovo.

Don Giuseppe had not proceeded far when the near shouts of his pursuers smote his ears. Distracted, he sprang into a hovel inhabited by a woman of ill fame, whose good faith he endeavoured to secure by lavish bribes. The woman feigned compliance for awhile, but as the desperadoes approached, either through cowardice or through hostility, betrayed the fugitive.

Don Giuseppe at once confronted his assailants. Not in this extremity of danger did his habitually haughty bearing forsake him. "*Che fate, canaglia*," he shouted. "Do you not know I am Don Giuseppe Carafa, and would you kill me?"

"It is just because you are a noble that we would do so," replied his opponents.

Don Giuseppe then tried the influence of bribery, and offered a costly reward if they would but spare his life. Threats, protests, and supplications were alike unheeded. His infuriated foes gave him but brief space for argument or entreaty, and the wretched Carafa saw with despair that his appeal for mercy was in vain.

"Plebeian dogs," he cried, as pierced by repeated sword thrusts he fell in mortal agony to the earth. One of his assassins, more brutal than the rest, immediately dissevered the head from the body. Such was the ignominious fate of the proud aristocrat who had formerly commanded one of these "plebeians" to kiss his feet in homage. Yet the man who exhibited this haughty insolence was habitually the companion of ruffians and adventurers, and though of illustrious descent and endowed with superior faculties and personal graces, he excelled the vilest in lawlessness and crime. The conduct of Don Giuseppe had not been less depraved and unscrupulous than that of Don Diomed Carafa himself. With such extravagant tyranny had the brothers ruled the territory under their sway, that Don Giuseppe had from mere ill temper caused three persons to be killed, and three others to be severely wounded, within the course of a day or two.* The tragic end of Don Giuseppe was a fearful retribution for those repeated crimes which had hitherto, through the connivance of a profligate government, remained unpunished.

Revolutions no less than religions demand their sacrifices. When an institution becomes unpopular an expiatory type is selected, upon

* Reumont's "Carafas of Maddaloni."

which falls the chastisement due to more than one. Centuries had witnessed the unblushing depravity of the Neapolitan aristocracy, and for centuries it had remained unpunished. The Revolution for the first time challenged these doers of evil, and justice visited the aristocratic order in sealing the fate of the man who was a representative of its vices.

The popular hatred of Carafa was shown in acts of inhuman ferocity degrading to their perpetrators. His body, dragged through the streets, was left without burial, but is supposed to have been afterwards secretly interred in consecrated ground by the pious charity of some unknown hand.* The head of Carafa, carried on the point of a spear through the city, amidst the opprobrious shouts of the mob, was finally enclosed within an iron cage, and placed at the gate of St Gennaro. A gilt crown, set in mockery on the head, increased the ghastliness of the spectacle.† An inscription underneath proclaimed it "the head of Don Giuseppe, the traitor and enemy of the people."‡

* Capecelatro, "Diario," p. 58.

† Capecelatro, "Diario," p. 57. Baldacchini, "Storia Napoletana," p. 79.

‡ Burana, "Batalla Peregrina," p. 136.

Since the unhappy hour of the Maddaloni conspiracy a tumult of passion, little else than frenzied, had filled the public mind. The masses who had been for ages plundered and enslaved, now turned on their oppressors, and the fire of their smouldering hate burst forth to be quenched in blood. Barbarities, it is true, they committed, yet these were in retaliation for the almost inconceivable cruelties which they had from time immemorial received at the hands of the privileged classes, whom they desired to annihilate. Scourged into the condition of outcasts by ruthless acts of power, and degraded into affinity with baseness of every kind as the lower classes of the Neapolitans had been, it is scarcely rational to suppose that they, more than others, emerging from a state of servitude, should have displayed the philosophic magnanimity of superior wisdom. "Our rigour relents," as Burke remarks, "and we pardon something to the exasperated Spirit of Liberty."

All Naples was again a prey to anarchy. Disorder and licence prevailed to a greater extent than at any period during the Revolution.

Discord, with the Furies in her train, appeared to have descended, and taken possession of the unhappy city. Blackened ruins marked the sites of once magnificent palaces. Uncouth revolutionary barricades encumbered the highways. Cannons were mounted in all directions, and everywhere the presence of the armed militia, or the populace wielding the savage weapons of sedition, presented a warlike and menacing aspect. Above all, the bodies of the unburied slain, in and about the market-place, offered a ghastly, revolting spectacle.

Yet only those had been sacrificed who had been guilty of the gravest crimes, and the populace, when reading the placards attached to the heads of the slain recording the offences for which they had suffered, exclaimed, "Thank Heaven we are rid of them."*

The Revolution had received a fresh impetus. A mad zeal for warfare appeared to have seized the minds of men, women, and children. Troops of armed peasants continued to pour into the town.† Women in Amazonian companies wielded guns, sticks, and pikes.

Peremptory orders were given out by Masaniello that the citizen troops should remain on the *qui vive*, and not leave a single fortification or intrenchment unguarded by night or day.

* Donzelli, "Partenope Liberata," p. 38.

† Capecelatro, "Diario," p. 59.

The effect of the terror which prevailed was to increase the authority of the soldiery, who had almost irresponsible power in their hands. We have seen that it was the common practice of the wealthy to endeavour to secure their riches by entrusting them to the keeping of the monks. Either for the discovery of secreted property, therefore, or for the capture of banditti, the soldiery had free access alike to cathedral, convent, or palace.

Masaniello, to prevent the occurrence of deeds of violence during a time of such intense excitement, issued a decree prohibiting the *mezza sottana*, or priestly robe, which, as we have seen, was in Naples so frequently the cloak for nefarious practices, and afforded a means of concealment for fire-arms and weapons, which it was forbidden to carry in secret. Large cloaks and mantles, and even the capacious hooped skirts of women, then as now the pride of fashion, were for the same reason forbidden.* The Cardinals Filomarino and Trivulzio laid aside their robes for a time, out of deference to the proclamation of Masaniello, which was universally obeyed. The various religious orders of Naples were seen

* Baldacchini, "Storia Napoletana," p. 81.

in quaint procession, having their flowing draperies gathered up within their girdles, and bearing staffs in their hands after the manner of pilgrims. Masaniello commanded the inhabitants of the city to keep lamps or torches burning during the night before their dwellings. They were ordered also to mount the royal arms on the right of their houses, and on the left the insignia of the people.

No one was permitted, under the severest penalty, to quit the city without the sanction of Masaniello.

Diligent efforts were made to defend the fortifications from the assaults of the Spaniards and banditti, and barricades were carefully erected across the leading thoroughfares, to guard against sorties of the Royal troops from the Castle.

The Duke of Arcos was impatient under the increasing perplexity of his position. Revolution raged within the State. With craven-hearted troops, fortresses unprovisioned, and courtiers who were fugitives or captives, execrated personally and characteristically feeble—such was the unenviable position of the Viceroy. What if the foreign enemy, taking advantage of the crisis, should turn against him in league with the furious foe within the city? The rule of the Angevins had not departed without leaving a bias of French blood in the veins of the citizens. The tide of insurrection had been strengthened, not stemmed, by the conspiracy of Maddaloni. The Duke of Arcos now perceived the fatal error of having in secret favoured the design, though, with his habitual duplicity, he had contrived to act so as not to publicly inculpate himself in the transaction. In this dilemma he had recourse to his invariable expedient of unscrupulous cowardice, deception, and intrigue. He again referred to the mediation of Cardinal Filomarino,* and in a letter full of perfidious declarations, assured the Cardinal of his fervent wishes for the welfare of the State, and of his bitter regret that the hopes of peace had been frustrated by so infamous a plot. He continued by expressing his approval of the right of search accorded to the soldiery for the discovery of bandits, and declared his resolve to surrender to the people as many as should fall into the hands of the royal party.†

The efforts of Filomarino meanwhile were unabated, in order to ensure a return of peace.

* Capecelatro, "Diario," p. 59.

† Baldacchini, "Storia Napoletana," p. 82.

By day and night, hurrying from castle to palace, and from palace to market-place, now arguing with revolutionists, and now with royalists, conciliation was his constant aim. He even consented to give his blessing to the people from the Campanile of the Carmine, a concession which greatly scandalized the Spaniards, who declared he thus sought to sanctify the Revolution.

CHAPTER X.

NOTWITHSTANDING the negotiations so vigorously carried on by Cardinal Filomarino for the conclusion of peace, the agitation and tumult which had been occasioned by the conspiracy still occasioned fresh disorders in the city.

The insurgents, unsuccessful in tracking the fugitive Diomed Carafa, revenged themselves on their enemy by the sack of his palace and the destruction of his sumptuous possessions.* A portion of these had been deposited within the adjacent monastery of Santa Maria della Stella, but these were dragged forth at the command of the insurgents. The abundant wealth of the Counts of Maddaloni had enabled them to indulge to the utmost in the extravagant love of

* Nicolai, "Historia del ultime Rivolutioni di Napoli," p. 72.

display that characterized the aristocracy of Naples; and the destruction of Don Diomed's possessions constituted one of the most costly sacrifices of the Revolution.

Masaniello, in order still more to cripple the resources of the nobility, called upon them to surrender the majority of their retainers and whatever fire-arms they owned, for the public service. The order was in some cases complied with, but in many instances, notwithstanding the severe penalty imposed on disobedience of the command, the reply returned was that "the tumult of the times had left the nobles little else than their persons and their swords, and the last was quite necessary to protect the first." *

Upon the arrival of the fleet under Doria in the Neapolitan gulf, Masaniello sent orders to the Admiral that it should not approach within a mile of the shore. The command was obeyed, and a single official only was sent on land for the purpose of offering formal salutation to Masaniello as ruler of Naples, and to request that he would forward to the fleet the supplies of which it was so much in need. Masaniello

* Baldacchini, "Storia Napoletana," p. 84.

had repaired to his usual place of audience to receive the Admiral's messenger, who was not a little astonished to see in the humbly-attired fisherman, seated on a rude platform, the sovereign ruler of the Neapolitans.

Masaniello not only forwarded an abundance of provisions to Doria's fleet, but, generous to his worst enemies, when told of the deprivation which the garrison of a certain fortress held by the Royalists had to endure owing to want of food, sent them a plentiful supply of bread.*

The Viceroy, encouraged by this clemency on the part of Masaniello, perceiving, moreover, the hesitation on the part of the people again to trust the faith of Spaniards, and fearful of the fresh disorders which would ensue from delay in ratifying the peace, again addressed Cardinal Filomarino, urging him to hasten the arrangements necessary to the conclusion of the treaty. Masaniello, anxious to secure the quietude of the State, informed the Viceroy of his desire to enter into an agreement with him. The Duke of Arcos again wrote to Filomarino, desiring him to assure the people and their leader of his willingness to enter entirely into their wishes.

* Capecelatro, "Diario," p. 62.

The several clauses of the treaty were then drawn up by Masaniello and Genuino.* These were to be publicly read in the Carmelite Cathedral.

There, upon this occasion, a rich dais was prepared beneath a magnificent canopy, where the Cardinal in full pontifical robes took his place. Seated at a little distance were Masaniello, Genuino, and the newly-elected Deputy of the people, Arpaia.† The aisles and galleries of the sacred building were filled to excess. The articles of agreement were then read aloud, and no sooner had the voice of the notary ceased, than the solemn peal of the organ arose, and a hymn of grateful devotion ascended from the thousand voices of the assembly. Now the time of long-desired repose had surely come, bringing a glad reprieve from tumults, treacheries, and grief.

The Viceroy, with the view professedly of cementing the negotiations, desired that a conference should take place between himself and Masaniello, after which the peace should be declared with public ceremony in the Carmelite Cathedral, when the Viceroy should take a solemn oath to observe

* Capecelatro, "Diario," p. 65.

† De Santis, "Historia di Napoli," p. 107.

the Charter.* Not without deep meditation and reference to the expressed wishes of the people, did Masaniello consent to an interview with the Viceroy. His mind was filled with strange forebodings, and for the first time a presentiment of evil oppressed the intrepid heart of the fisherman. He reflected on his originally humble position, and on the momentous work he had dared to achieve. Would the power he had outraged pardon the author of such innovation? Had not the Spaniards already perfidiously sought his downfall and the destruction of his hopes? It were scarcely possible that another sentiment than deadly hatred lurked under the simulated cordialities of the Viceroy. If it were not the torture and the gibbet which he had to fear, there were other secret and not less certain methods of destruction in those days by which the powerful did not scruple to sacrifice stumbling-blocks in their path. He confessed his apprehensions to the Cardinal Filomarino, who used his utmost influence to persuade him to consent to the interview.† Masaniello determined to abide by the expressed will of his people, the majority of whom con-

* Capecelatro, "Diario," p. 65.

† Baldacchini, "Storia Napoletana," p. 91.

sented to the conference. Masaniello, then placing his hand over his face, as he was accustomed to do when absorbed in reflection, resolved to visit the Duke of Arcos, on condition that the meeting should take place in the palace, and not in the castle.

In accordance with the order of Masaniello, an estimate was published of the number of the revolutionary forces, according to which three hundred thousand* were reckoned available for action, provided that they were supplied with sufficient arms for their equipment. It is difficult—perhaps impossible—to arrive at a correct calculation of the forces under Masaniello's command, though, from a comparison of the estimates given by various writers, we are enabled, doubtless, to obtain a result proximate to the truth. Giannone mentions a hundred and forty thousand as taking part in the rebellion at one period. Capecelatro, the most accurate and impartial chronicler of the insurrection, records that two thousand took part in it at the outbreak of the revolt on the 7th of July, and that the numbers speedily increased to a motley throng of double the amount, until on the 9th day the revolutionary forces ex-

* Capecelatro, "Diario," p. 65.

ceeded a hundred thousand. The Tuscan Ducal agents resident in Naples mention a hundred and fifty thousand as under arms.*

On the occasion of Masaniello's visit to the palace, the citizen troops lined the ways from the market-place to the castle. "An infinite number of well-ordered bands," writes a quaint contemporary chronicler of the insurrection, "combining unity of spirit and excellent discipline, with martial ardour, congregated under their respective standards."

The entire city wore a triumphal aspect, in honour of the eventful occasion of the conference. The squares and streets through which the procession attending Masaniello intended to pass were thoroughly cleansed. The houses, draped with rich tapestries from basement to roof, or garlanded with flowers, appeared a mass of emblazonry. Countless banners gleamed in the light, which flashed on the steel-crested ranks of the soldiery. An eager concourse thronged every quarter of the city.†

But the soul of Masaniello was little in unison with the gratulation and homage of which he

* Archivio Storico Italiano, vol. ix.

† Baldacchini, "Storia Napoletana," p. 93.

was the object. He had entreated the Cardinal Filomarino to give him absolution previous to his visit. His request was, however, denied by the Cardinal, either owing to his distrust of Masaniello's expressed desire for peace, or because he imagined the thoughts of the poor fisherman were too entirely absorbed in earthly speculations to render it a fitting moment for such a ceremony. Filomarino promised ample absolution, however, as soon as the treaty should be concluded.*

Masaniello had entertained the idea of visiting the Duke of Arcos in his ordinary garb of white linen. Thus attired, the simple-hearted fisherman had presented himself to the Cardinal and his suite, who awaited him, but upon his arrival remonstrated with him upon the unfitness of his apparel. To this Masaniello replied, "it was the dress of his class, the one in which he had fought for the rights of the people, and the only one he should ever wear with pride or look upon with pleasure." His judgment and his taste alike rejected rich array or illustrious titles, for Masaniello neither courted honours nor desired display. He knew how transient and de-

* De Santis, "Historia di Napoli," p. 110.

ceptive were the favours of Fortune, and he despised them ere they forsook him. He stedfastly refused exaltation of every kind. When addressed as "Illustrious Excellency," he exclaimed, "Stay, such titles do not become me. My name is that of the poor Fisherman, Masaniello." *

Filomarino encountered the greatest difficulty, consequently, in the task of persuading Masaniello to exchange his humble attire for the rich suit which the Cardinal had provided, of cloth of silver —white, denoting peace. Masaniello, out of deference to ecclesiastical authority, upon the repeated solicitations of Filomarino, at length consented to clothe himself in the costly apparel.† A velvet hat, ornamented by a white plume, completed his costume. Thus attired, riding a white horse with his sword at his side, and wearing on his breast a medallion of the Madonna, he is portrayed in a picture by the hand of his friend, Micco Spadaro.

Masaniello rode, during the procession to the palace, at the right hand of the Cardinal's carriage, which contained Filomarino, Genuino, and

* Botta, "Storia d'Italia," vol. vi. p. 329. De Santis, "Historia di Napoli," p. 110.

† Capecelatro, "Diario," p. 66. Tarsia, "Tumultos de la Ciudad de Napoles," p. 71.

several of the Cardinal's suite. On the left rode Arpaia, Deputy of the people.

Eager faces thronged the thoroughfares. All were anxious to witness the remarkable spectacle. The *vivas* of the excited multitude and the sounds of martial music filled the air. The troops lowered their colours as their Captain-General passed. So dense was the mass of people, that the cavalcade, at one point, could not proceed. Masaniello then raised himself in the stirrups so as to be seen by the entire assembly. The look and action were sufficient to indicate his meaning, and the crowd instantly fell back, leaving the way unimpeded.*

In the square adjacent to the palace were placed, under State canopies, portraits of the Emperor Charles V. and the reigning monarch of Spain.† Masaniello, advancing in front of these, addressed the people, and showed them the document of the Imperial Charter which he carried with him. He declared that everything was now arranged for the ratification of the peace, and he entreated them to believe that the public welfare had been the sole object of his

* Donzelli, "Partenope Liberata," p. 51.

† Capecelatro, "Diario," p. 66.

exertions, as the gratitude of the populace should be his only recompense. The people replied that "all he had done was done well, and that they were more than content."

Masaniello continued, that he blushed to appear in such gaudy array, but he had assumed it out of deference to the Church and her dignitaries. "For me," he exclaimed, "I am about to trust myself into the hands of the king's representative, and ere I go, I pray his Eminence to give us all his Holy Benediction." Cardinal Filomarino then waved his hands, by way of assent, over the heads of the people.

Masaniello then entered at a rapid pace within the square of the palace. Here he was received with military honours by the guards, who invited him in the name of the Viceroy to enter. The entrance of the square was kept by the Spanish infantry, and so strictly barricaded that a very narrow passage only was left, through which the Cardinal's carriage had some difficulty in passing.* Though the occasion was avowedly the inauguration of peace, everything in the vicinity of the palace denoted war. At the gate of the old palace of Pietro di Toledo, ramparts of earth

* Capecelatro, "Diario," p. 67.

had been thrown up, and the opposite height of Pizzofalcone,* guarded by a regiment of Italian infantry under Field-marshal Tuttavilla, was strongly fortified and entrenched. The great gate of the new palace itself was powerfully defended. In the court-yard, filled with Spaniards, Germans, and Walloons, the mounted cannon pointed towards the outer entrance. Masaniello, surveying these martial preparations around him, again turned and addressed the multitude. "My people," he exclaimed, "if by the midnight hour you do not see me come forth, do not let one stone remain upon another on this spot."† Then, more pious reflections filling his mind, he continued, "If I should perish, promise me to repeat an Ave for my soul." The people replied that "all should be as he desired." ‡

The Viceroy meanwhile stood in one of the saloons of the palace awaiting the deputation. Masaniello, upon meeting the Duke of Arcos, knelt at his feet. The Duke raising him up with the most friendly salutation, embraced him.§ The Viceroy then repaired with Cardinal Filomarino

* De Santis, "Historia di Napoli," p. 76.

† Ibid. p. 111.

‡ Baldacchini, "Storia Napoletana," p. 94.

§ Botta, "Storia d'Italia," vol. vi. p. 328.

and Masaniello to the Royal Hall, where he again embraced Masaniello, and renewed his assurances of cordiality.

The populace, meanwhile, anxious not to lose sight of the movements of their leader, had thronged the square and the court-yard in such numbers that the troops were unable to restrain them. This increasing tumult was perceived by the Duke of Arcos, who begged of Masaniello to appear in one of the balconies, and, if possible, disperse the people.

"I will obey your Excellency's command," replied Masaniello.* Accompanied by the Viceroy, he then appeared in one of the balconies of the palace. The Viceroy then embraced him in sight of the assembled multitude, and lauded him as the Deliverer of the People.†

"I am here, my friends," cried Masaniello. These words, with an accompanying pressure of the finger on the lips, symbolic of silence, immediately stilled the commotion among the crowd, when Masaniello, turning to the Viceroy, exclaimed, "See how easily they might be governed!"

* Donzelli, "Partenope Liberata," p. 51.

† Baldacchini, Storia Napoletana," p. 95.

Not without reason were the Neapolitans disquieted by fears for their leader. Notwithstanding the affected friendliness of the Duke, the evil intentions he certainly entertained towards Masaniello were restrained from immediate fulfilment solely through fear of the populace. He, who trembled to see the court-yard of his palace crowded, had not the audacity to infuriate his enemies still further. Perfidy of the darkest dye lurked under his caresses and cordialities.

Upon returning into the saloon which he had first entered, Masaniello was suddenly attacked with illness.* The strange vicissitudes he had experienced and the scenes he had witnessed, the excitement of incessant action and discourse, the denial of necessary food and rest—all had concurred to exhaust his bodily powers. A shadow of the approaching eclipse passed over the unhappy patriot. He lost for awhile his senses and his speech. A cold damp, as of the last mortal agony, covered him, and he lay in a swoon so profound as to appear like death.†

The Viceroy was scared with terror. He trembled for his own life if Masaniello, the

* De Santis, "Historia di Napoli," p. 112.

† Capecelatro, "Diario," p. 68.

darling of the people, should die whilst in his presence. He tended him assiduously, and wiped the damp from his brow with his own handkerchief.*

The populace had again gathered in large numbers at the entrance to the palace. The sense of deference on the part of the people to the will of Masaniello had given way before their renewed fears for his safety. Upon the recovery of Masaniello, therefore, the Duke entreated him a second time to appear before the people. He consented. At a sign from Masaniello the crowd again dispersed.

Masaniello, with the Viceroy and Cardinal Filomarino, then withdrew to the Council Chamber, where the articles of the agreement which had been drawn up were discussed and mutually accepted. The conference was at an end, and the Viceroy consented that a public declaration of the treaty should take place two days subsequently in the Carmelite Cathedral, where he would bind himself by a solemn oath to observe all the conditions of the compact.† The title of Captain-General of the People, the only one Masaniello

* Baldacchini, "Storia Napoletana," p. 75.

† Ibid. p. 96.

would consent to adopt, was confirmed by the Viceroy, who pressed Masaniello to accept a costly jewel. This was stedfastly refused,* but upon the solicitations of the Cardinal, who seconded the Duke's request, Masaniello accepted a small gold chain of little value.

Masaniello, then kissing the Viceroy's hand, quitted the presence of his deadliest enemy. The procession departed from the Palace in the same order in which it had arrived. Night was closing in as the cavalcade wended its way through the city, which, draped and decorated, glowed in the vivid light cast by innumerable lamps and torches. The tramp of feet, the hum of voices, and the sounds of music, were unceasing. All Naples rejoiced as on a gala night: it was a Carnival of Patriotism.

Masaniello, the hero of the triumph, returned to his humble dwelling on the market-place, and resumed his simple garb as a Fisherman.

* Botta, "Storia d'Italia," vol. vi. p. 329.

CHAPTER XI.

Masaniello continued to direct his attention to the more complete organization of the militia, which he regarded as an object of the first importance in the present crisis of the national affairs. During the three months which had to elapse before the ratification of the treaty by the Court of Madrid, the people were to remain armed.* It was imperative in that critical season, therefore, that an effectual check should exist to restrain the outrages of conspirators and traitors with bandits in their train. The military companies of the Conciaria were accordingly entrusted to the bold leadership of Giuseppe Palumba. The detachments of the busy Lavinario were committed to the care of Matteo

* Capecelatro, "Diario."

d'Amore, and those of the market quarter were submitted to Gennaro Annese, a name afterwards famous in the later annals of the Neapolitan Revolution.

An edict was issued by Masaniello prohibiting the existing monoply in oil, of which there was a dearth in the city, and the same proclamation forbade the absence of the citizens after the midnight hour from their dwellings except in cases of urgent necessity. Those in attendance on the sick, or pastors called upon to administer the last rites of the Church, were exempted.

The crusade against the banditti continued in full force.* Churches and monasteries were still searched in pursuit of them, and capital punishment was the sentence passed on those who sheltered such fugitives. No quarter was shown to the numbers who were taken captive. They were conducted without trial to the scaffold erected for their execution, where they met with the recompense of those crimes from which the power of their wealthy patrons had hitherto shielded them.

Petitioners thronged to the simple audience seat of the ruler of Naples, and not content with

* Capecelatro, "Diario," p. 71.

crowding the platform, presented the memorials of their grievances or requests on the points of halberts or pikes through the low windows of Masaniello's little house on the market-place. Among these was one presented by a Spanish soldier, stating that he was infirm and in extreme want, without a resting-place or a bed to lie upon. Masaniello ordered a suitable habitation to be provided for him, and gave him a liberal sum of money. Masaniello showed equal benevolence in his acts of charity to poor women, whom he drew from a life of infamy and indigence by his liberality in granting them money and such possessions as should enable them to live honestly.*

If magnanimous in showing generosity, he was severe in awarding justice. Imposture, above all, he treated with harshness. A young fisherman of the Chiaja, under the pretence that he was a relative of Masaniello, had succeeded in extorting money from several persons. Masaniello, indignant at the fraud committed in his name, imprisoned the young man, and made restitution of the money to those who had been robbed.†

* Capecelatro, "Diario," p. 74.

† Botta, "Storia d'Italia," vol. vi. p. 350.

The substance of the treaty of peace, which was about to be ratified in the Carmelite Cathedral, promised important reforms to the State. All the taxes which had been imposed since the grant of the Charter by Charles V. were abolished, and the arbitrary introduction of fresh ones was prohibited.* The plebeians were accorded equality of votes with the nobles. A declaration which, as we have seen, was scouted by the haughty insurgents, proclaimed a free pardon for all past offences. Masaniello now fondly hoped that he had brought to a termination the work which had been desired for centuries by all those interested in reform. The ancient rights of the city were about to be restored, the overbearing pride of the nobles would be suppressed, and the voice of the people would be heard in the discussion of their own affairs. And this had been achieved by a single invincible will, seconded by the power of an enthusiastic people. If Masaniello had shown himself severe, it was towards the enemies of his country alone. The blood which had been shed was drawn from the corrupt body of the State to ensure its restoration to health. Concession was extorted

* Giannone, "Storia de Napoli," Lib. xxxvii.

through fear only because it would not be yielded in justice. If it should be objected that the work accomplished by Masaniello rested on a weak foundation, and that he had gained only a compact of words, yet this, confirmed by a solemn oath, was all which it was possible to obtain, and would have sufficed had it not been sworn to by traitors.

CHAPTER XII.

Naples wore a festive aspect as the hour approached for the solemnization of the peace in the venerable cathedral of the city. Bright-hued banners, pennons, and rich tapestries once more glowed in the light. Joyful peals of triumph rang out from the belfries, and mingled with the stirring sound of trumpets and the beat of drums. Armed masses lined the streets through which the procession was to pass, as before on the occasion of Masaniello's visit to the palace. The nobles and gentlemen of the city kept guard, as they had been called upon to do, at the thresholds of their houses.

The Viceroy was accompanied in his magnificent carriage only by a few subordinate members of his court. In the first detachment of the procession, with the Duke of Arcos, rode Deputy Arpaia, the new Elect of the People, and the ruthless traitor, Genuino, whom the Viceroy had now created, in return for his secret services, Prèsident of the Royal Chamber.

As the cavalcade proceeded on its way, cries of "Long live the Duke of Arcos, long live the King," rent the air.* By one of those swift but baneful re-actions which universally characterize the populace, the too credulous Neapolitans now showered blessings on the man whom they had so recently execrated. The Viceroy, in the blandest manner, acknowledged their expressions of loyalty with repeated salutations.†

Upon the arrival of the Duke of Arcos at the entrance of the cathedral, he was joined by Masaniello, who, attired in cloth of silver, and on horseback, was followed by a dense crowd shouting enthusiastic plaudits of their Chief. At tho doors of the sacred edifice he dismounted, and knelt at the feet of the Viceroy, who, raising Masaniello with cordial friendliness, embraced him.

Within the cathedral the Viceroy was received

* Capecelatro, "Diario," p. 75.

† Baldacchini, "Storia Napoletana," p. 102.

by the Royal chaplains, and in accordance with the usual custom, he was sprinkled by them with the holy water.* This office performed, the chaplains were about to retire, when the Duke signified to them to administer the rite to Masaniello also, which they did.†

Cardinal Filomarino, arrayed in full Pontifical attire, awaited the arrival of the Viceroy within the cathedral. Masaniello, approaching His Eminence, knelt reverently at his feet, but the Cardinal, with the urbane demeanour habitual to him, smiled and raised him up.‡ Filomarino then took his seat under the canopy which had been prepared for him.

At a little distance were stationed the Duke of Arcos and Masaniello, and Donato Coppola, Secretary of State. The captains of the city districts, the counsellors of the People's Piazza, those of the Collateral Council, andof the Royal Chamber were present, and before the entire assembly the Viceroy took a solemn oath of allegiance to the Charter.§ The several deputies then thanked him in the name of the citizens.

* De Santis, "Historia di Napoli," p. 124.

† Donzelli, "Partenope Liberata," p. 53. ‡ Ibid.

§ De Santis, "Historia di Napoli," p. 132. Botta, "Storia d'Italia," vol. vi. p. 327.

Some authors have ingeniously sought to excuse the violation of this solemn compact by the Viceroy. More conscientious writers should not shrink from branding the name of the Duke of Arcos as that of a perjured traitor and coward.

Upon the conclusion of the ceremony in the cathedral, the glorious *Laudamus* echoed through the sacred edifice.* The multitude without caught up the triumphal sounds, and shouted joyous *vivas* as the citizen companies without discharged their fire-arms in honour of the event.†

As the Duke of Arcos left the cathedral, accompanied by Cardinal Filomarino and Deputy Arpaia to his carriage, Masaniello threw his sword on the ground before the Viceroy, and announced to the surrounding multitude that he was now again the Poor Fisherman, and that they no longer owed obedience to him, but only to the Viceroy. The Duke, apparently gratified by this surrender of authority, again embraced Masaniello. As the Viceroy returned through the crowded streets, he was everywhere gladly welcomed. His treachery had secured him a transient popularity.

* Antonio de Sarsia, "Tumultos de la Ciudad de Napoles," p. 75.

† Capecelatro, "Diario," pp. 84, 85.

CHAPTER XIII.

Rejoicings in celebration of the peace continued on the following day. Fêtes were held at Posilippo, and also at Poggio Reale. This delicious spot was a favourite resort of the Neapolitans during the 17th century, and amidst the perfume, foliage, and flowers of its exquisite gardens, aristocrats lounged and citizens reposed, seeking refreshment in their shades from the turmoil and heat of the city. Here, too, some of the more kindly rulers of Naples had been accustomed to give rustic feasts to the people. Among the entertainments now initiated by the Viceroy in celebration of the national rejoicing was an excursion by water to Posilippo, in which Masaniello joined. A still more animated procession than that of the preceding day was the graceful train of gondolas which sped swiftly and buoyantly over the

Neapolitan waters. Numerous vessels followed that of the Duke of Arcos. A vast concourse had assembled to witness the spectacle, and the chants of the boatmen rose on the air, mingled with echoes from the shore, of glad voices, with songs and shouts recording the praises of the Fisherman of Naples.

But again the soul of the ill-fated Masaniello was overshadowed. Destiny had stamped its irresistible presentiments on his heart, which asked how long would these admiring plaudits endure? It was a critical period in the life of the leader of the Neapolitan Revolution. His power was at its zenith. A series of momentous events had been crowded with unparalleled rapidity into his brief career, and heroic achievements, which would have sufficed for the labour of a life, had in a few short days rendered the name of Masaniello illustrious. The trials he had undergone, the exciting scenes he had witnessed, his perpetual watchfulness and diligence, the want of sleep and nourishment, with the exhaustion produced by the summer heat of the south,—all were injurious influences, and told with doubly destructive force upon his nervous and highly-strung temperament. These causes are, perhaps, sufficient to account for the morbid condition of mind which impelled Masaniello to commit acts of recklessness and cruelty so foreign to his nature as to be explicable only through the fact of his madness; a fact universally acknowledged by chroniclers of the Revolution.* Or are we to look for the source of this madness itself in the dark suggestion invariably contained in the pages of these chroniclers themselves?

In those days, however unripe the science of medicine in the exercise of healing properties and restorative powers, a profound and subtle knowledge existed among the Italians of the terrible art by means of which life and reason might speedily be destroyed. So common, indeed, was the use of poison in Italy at that date, that almost invariably cases of sudden death were attributed, and too often with justice, to its effects. The deadly essence was conveyed though numberless channels, and lurked as a canker under the form of objects the most familiar and pleasant. A bouquet of flowers, a trinket, a sweetmeat, a cosmetic, or a letter, contained perhaps its malignant and irresistible influence. One of

* Donzelli, "Partenope Liberata," p. 61. Baldacchini, "Storia Napoletana," p. 113. Botta, "Storia d' Italia," p. 331. Nicolai, "Historia del ultime Rivolutioni di Napoli," p. 77. Tontoli, "Il Masaniello," p. 138.

the most singular and terrible features which characterized the art in that age was the quality discovered in a certain poison, by which the human reason could be destroyed while life still remained to the victim of its operations. An unpleasant echo rings from page to page of various writers significant of the conviction that Masaniello was poisoned. The interchange of presents between him and the Duke of Arcos, as well as their partaking of refreshments together, afforded the Viceroy ample opportunity for thus disposing of his enemy. More than one author affirms that a bunch of poisoned flowers was sent by the Duke to Masaniello. By others it is asserted that a deadly beverage was given to him on the occasion of the excursion to Posilippo, when Masaniello accompanied the Viceroy in his gondola, in which a sumptuous repast of wines, fruits, and sweetmeats was prepared. The symptoms evinced by Masaniello immediately subsequent to this excursion* certainly lead to the inference of his having been poisoned there. He was parched with thirst, and drank an almost incredible amount of water.† Nothing availed

* Burana, "Batalla Peregrina," p. 157.

† Baldacchini, "Storia Napoletana," p. 109.

to quench the burning heat with which he suffered, and tortured with inward fever, he tried in delirious frenzy to fling himself, clothed as he was, into the sea. His mental aberration was unmistakeable, and showed itself, as is frequently the case, in the exhibition of qualities and sentiments utterly at variance with those which had hitherto distinguished him. He now gave way to capricious childish acts, and to deeds of positive ferocity. If a crowd of people chanced to displease him by some triviality, he attacked them indiscriminately with whatever weapon he happened to have at his command. He threatened to expel those who lived near his cottage in the market-place if they did not vacate their dwellings within the space of twenty-four hours, in order to allow room for the erection of a suitable palace for himself. He squandered money and distributed lavishly mock titles. He no longer spoke of remaining in obscurity, nor of resigning command, nor did he invite the assent of the people to his measures, as before. He was now unable to find the repose of which—absorbed in labours for his country—he had hitherto deprived himself. During his sleepless nights he would open the windows of his dwelling and shout incoherent menaces and commands. To such indignities did the unhappy Masaniello unconsciously descend.

The atrocious aim of the Viceroy was now, in part, at least, accomplished. He saw with satisfaction his dreaded and detested enemy, the victim of a doom more bitter than death. The hero of the Neapolitans so lately revered, applauded, and caressed, was now becoming odious in the sight of his beloved people. The Duke was so far successful. The most important obstacle to his base design was removed. Masaniello once rendered unpopular, the rest could with impunity be realized. He need no longer fear the vengeance of the people, whatever the fate in store for their once venerated leader.

Those for whom Masaniello had toiled, to whom he had devoted the entire energies of his soul, now in his dire need forsook and spurned him. The blight of ingratitude fell on the pure promise of his hope. Emoluments and honours which others would eagerly have grasped, he in his magnanimity had disdained and refused. One aspiration, one desire, sublime in its unselfishness, alone he had cherished, and this was denied. He had assured his people that his sole recompense should be their welfare, yet with his own abasement too surely and inevitably was associated the downfall of the popular party and the denial of reform.

A heart of charity towards the unhappy Masaniello beat in the breast of one alone amongst the many who surrounded him, and who had flattered him in the hour of pride and triumph. The benevolent Cardinal Filomarino endeavoured to restrain him from appearing in public,* and thus sought to shield Masaniello from the saddest evil consequent on his hapless condition, the ignominy of enduring the scorn and mockery of a capricious and heedless throng.

Malice, on the other hand, was busy at the work of detraction. The enemies of Masaniello, and above all the vile Genuino, did not fail by slanderous reports to heap still further opprobrium on his name. Genuino having received at the hands of the Viceroy the promotion he coveted,† at length threw off the mask of patriotism. His own interests served, he cared not how soon those of his country or its emancipator were sacrificed.

* Baldacchini, "Storia Napoletana," p. 114.

† "Capecelatro, "Diario," p. 86.

CHAPTER XIV.

A RUTHLESS destiny hovered over the ill-fated leader of the Revolution. The day preceding the festival of the Madonna of Carmel was devoted by the Viceroy to hastening the measures requisite for the execution of the plot against the life of Masaniello. The Duke of Arcos was warmly seconded in the foul scheme by Genuino, who now openly declared himself a traitor to the Revolution, and expressed the gratification he should derive from the destruction of Masaniello.

Leagued with the Duke of Arcos and Genuino were two ruffians, bearing the names of Michael Ardizzone and Salvatore Cateneo.* The Viceroy, in a conference with these assassins, or-

* De Santis, "Historia di Napoli," p. 144. Antonio de Tarsia, "Tumultos de la Ciudad de Naples," p. 92.

ganized the plot which was to be carried out on the following day of the festival* in honour of the Madonna. Arrangements were accordingly made during the night of the 15th. All the military posts were strengthened. Spanish troops were everywhere placed in ambush, and secretly lined the thoroughfares leading to the spot which was to be the scene of the conspiracy. The war vessels were brought in close proximity to the shore.†

The deadly work in hand was preceded by an act of ruffianism as gratuitous as it was dastardly. On the night of the 15th a message was sent to the Viceroy at the castle by Masaniello. Its delivery was entrusted to Marco Vitale, his secretary. Vitale was a young fellow of a noble spirit, devoted to his leader, and, like him, enthusiastic, but possessing little caution, and less experience. Vitale was destined to resemble him also in the cruel fate he met and the heroic memory he has left.

Vitale, when admitted to the castle, was artfully kept waiting, and denied direct communication with the Viceroy until a late hour

* Botta, "Storia d' Italia," vol. vi. p. 331.

† Baldacchini, "Storia Napoletana," p. 114.

of the night. By way of beguiling the time, he chatted with a group of courtiers, indiscreetly lauding the doings of Masaniello, and boasting proudly of what he yet intended to perform. At length, wearied and impatient, Vitale openly complained of the treatment he received, and resolved no longer to await the caprice of the Viceroy, but to depart at once. He found himself a prisoner—the bridge raised—the gates closed.

In order to re-assure the secretary, another reason was assigned by the inhabitants of the castle for these proceedings. The Viceroy now tried the influence of flattery and bribes to win the allegiance of Vitale to his cause and to bind him to secrecy. But repeated attempts failed to undermine the devotion of the secretary to his leader. The Duke of Arcos determined to ensure by force what he could not effect by stratagem. He resolved no revelation of what had passed at the castle should come from Vitale's lips, and kept him in close custody accordingly until his plans were matured.

Early in the morning Vitale, ignorant of the plot laid to ensnare him, took his leave. Incensed by the treatment he had received, he departed in an angry menacing mood, and made his way towards the Toledo quarter. Here he found armed squadrons assembled in accordance with the arrangements made by the Viceroy, and who awaited his instructions for further action. Vitale asked a captain of one of the companies by whose order they were assembled. The reply "by order of the Viceroy, who only in future should be obeyed," was given according to agreement by one of those in command, who was known as a personal enemy of Vitale's. The secretary, angry at the contempt thus thrown upon the authority of Masaniello, repaid insult for insult. All happened as had been anticipated. A haughty retort on the part of Vitale was the signal for his destruction. The captain who had answered him in the first instance now fired at him thrice, but missing his aim each time, hit him with brutal ferocity over the neck with his sword. Vitale, mortally wounded, fell and breathed his last sigh. Thus perished the unhappy man whose strange sad destiny preceded but by a few hours that of Masaniello himself. The body of Vitale was dragged through the streets,* and his head was paraded

* Nicolai, "Historia del ultime Rivolutioni di Napoli," p. 87.

on a lance. One faction indeed emulated another in barbarous ferocity, and whichever side was victorious gave humanity reason to feel shame for the use to which it turned success.

CHAPTER XV.

The day of the festival so devoutly celebrated by the Neapolitans in honour of the Lady of Carmel had arrived. The citizens, inspired by more than usual fervour, flocked to take part in the pious invocation of their protecting saint. It was the crowning consecration of their newly-found peace, and eager hopes ascended in prayer that celestial beneficence would guard the good work which it permitted human heroism to achieve.

As the Cardinal Filomarino entered the Carmelite Cathedral for the performance of the service, the sacred building was thronged with devotees* anxious to pour forth their supplication and praise at the shrine of the Virgin.

* De Santis, "Historia di Napoli," p. 147.

Masaniello was among the number, and scarcely had the high mass concluded than he ascended the pulpit for the purpose of discoursing to the assembly. At intervals reason again resumed her sway in the mind of Masaniello, but the transient light brought only anguish to his soul. With returning consciousness came all the bitterness of reality—the humiliating sense of ingratitude, abandonment, and desolation.

His devotion had been willingly rendered, his offences involuntarily committed. An ardent impulse now urged him to address his people. He desired to justify himself in their sight, and to recall, if possible, their wandering affection.

The burning words wrung from his heart's depths would surely find sympathetic response. At first he spoke with all his former eloquence, with the warmth which animates and the power which takes captive the popular feeling. He painted in bold and striking colours the dangers he had confronted, the mental toil he had endured in the service of his people, and expatiated on the benefits he had desired to confer upon them. "To do you this service," he continued, "I have banished sleep from my pillow, and have become so emaciated as to be truly an object of compassion."* At these touching words his hearers could not restrain their emotion. Masaniello had power once more to sway their spirits—they wept as they listened.

But the returning flash of intellect was swiftly quenched in darkness. Masaniello, forgetful, in returning aberration, of the sanctity of the place and the solemnity of the occasion, was about to undress in order to prove to the people how emaciated he had become for their sakes.†

The monks with pious care now interfered, and soon succeeded in persuading Masaniello to retire with them into the adjacent convent. There they gently tended him, soothing his excitement, and consoling him with kindly words, until at length, overcome with fatigue and emotion, he fell asleep.‡ In the quietude of a monastic cell the last moments of calm on earth were granted to Masaniello.

Upon awakening from a short slumber his mind appeared again to have recovered its balance. He stood for a few moments immoveable, in the attitude of one lost in deep and sorrowful reflec-

* Baldacchini, "Storia Napoletana," p. 117.

† "Diario" di Capecelatro, p. 95.

‡ Baldacchini, "Storia Napoletana," p. 118.

tion, looking down from out the high window of the convent cell, with his gaze fixed upon the sea. Contemplating the mighty element, majestic in its changeless glory, adoration of the Infinite filled his soul, and he was wrapt in sublime aspiration for the eternal repose. In those waters which the fisherman had so often braved, there was less inconstancy and treachery than in the men whom he had trusted and endeavoured to serve.

While thus absorbed in thought, unarmed, defenceless, and unsuspecting, Masaniello was sought by the base hirelings of the Viceroy, who had remained until this moment concealed in the cathedral. The assassins, Salvatore and Carlo Cateneo, Angelo Ardizzone and Andrea Rama—names for ever branded with infamy—now hurried in the direction of the cell where Masaniello was sheltered.* Fit agents of the Spanish traitor they served, their villany was cloaked to the last moment by deceit. Professing to seek Masaniello in order to discuss some important public matter, they called upon him repeatedly by name in a friendly tone.† Masaniello, imagining his adherents

* Antonio de Tarsia, "Tumultos de la Ciudad de Napoles," p. 93.

† Giraffi, "Rivolutioni di Napoli," p. 189.

to be in search of him, turned towards his pursuers with cordial aspect, as he exclaimed, "Do you seek me? I am here; perhaps my people are again in need of me." At these words the deadly aim of the destroyers was taken. Shot after shot was fired in quick succession. Masaniello, mortally wounded, fell to the earth,* covering his face with his hands, as he cried, "Traitors, ingrates,"† and was silent for ever. The voice which had so often sounded in defence of liberty, was heard no more. The name of the patriot of Naples alone remained as a reproach to tyrants. Cataneo, who had been bribed to do the ruthless deed, then smote the head from the body,‡ and the conspirators, hurrying swiftly and secretly away, joined some Spanish troops.

Cataneo then hastened with the bleeding head of the slaughtered man to the Viceroy,§ who expressed his delight in extravagant terms. The Duke could dispense with hypocrisy now that Masaniello was no longer his rival, but his victim;

* De Santis, "Historia di Napoli," p. 140.

† Baldacchini, "Storia Napoletana," p. 112. Burana, "Batalla Peregrina," p. 178.

‡ Capecelatro, "Diario," p. 96.

§ De Santis, "Historia di Napoli," p. 146. Botta, "Storia d'Italia," vol. vi. p. 332.

and he openly rejoiced on witnessing the ghastly trophy of his crime—a crime which would henceforth stigmatize the name of the Duke of Arcos as the instigator of an act of barbarity unsurpassed by the most flagrant deeds of iniquity which have ever darkened the annals of history.

Cardinal Filomarino, upon receiving news of the doom of Masaniello, immediately repaired to the Royal Palace. Here at the same time arrived the widow of the dead patriot. The unhappy woman, terror-stricken and distracted with grief, lamented aloud, and threw herself at the feet of the Cardinal, imploring his pity and protection. Never in vain did the unfortunate or oppressed appeal to his gracious heart. Through the mediation of the Cardinal, the wife and sister of Masaniello were shielded from the miseries attending the desolation into which they were plunged, and were spared the contempt and neglect of the many who, having flattered them in their exaltation, would infallibly spurn them in their abasement. They were lodged suitably for awhile under the protection of the Cardinal, and ultimately retired into a convent.*

The Neapolitans had yet to realize the irre-

* Baldacchini, "Storia Napoletana," p. 121.

parable loss they had sustained in the death of their chief. The bold policy of the Viceroy in the destruction of his enemy, and the suddenness and audacity of the means by which his downfall had been effected, appeared to have effectually suppressed for the time the national will. The people, relapsing from their recent ebullition of enthusiasm, now seemed to regard with utter insensibility and indifference the outrage upon their liberty in the unscrupulous sacrifice of its defender. Those who had clamoured at the shadow of peril approaching their benefactor, and who had followed the track of his footsteps with blessings, now beheld with supineness, irreverence offered to his remains, which were dragged through the streets by some ruffianly hirelings of the Spaniards.

No sooner were the people left without a champion, than they were oppressed anew. The price of bread was raised at once as a preparatory step to the violation of other promises of benefits supposed to be secured to the community by the viceregal oath.

The citizens openly murmured at this, and the Viceroy trembled lest a reaction should take place. Already, a strong revulsion of feeling was displayed. A sense of remorse for their apathy speedily stirred the hearts of the people, who, with tears and cries, lamented the loss of their benefactor, Masaniello. The head of the fallen patriot, which had been exposed by the malignity of his enemies as an object of derision in the public ways, was now placed with the body,* which received the last rites of mortality. Then, arrayed in befitting garments, it was laid in state in the Carmelite Cathedral. Eager throngs hurried once again to do homage to the hero of Naples. Flowers wet with the tears of women were strewn as pious offerings over his remains. Masaniello had become a saint in the popular sight.† They were envied who succeeded amidst the crowd in kissing his foot, or his hand, or in cherishing as a relic a single lock of his hair. Supplicants for charity at the church gates asked, "for whom shall we repeat an *ave?* for the soul of the blessed Masaniello."‡ Unmeasured enthusiasm had succeeded to momentary apathy. It was useless, if not dangerous, for rulers to contend against this demonstration of the national feeling.

Accordingly on the night of the 17th of July, the obsequies were celebrated with solemn pomp.

* Botta, "Storia d'Italia," vol. vi. p. 332.

† Tarsia, "Tumultos de la Ciudad de Napoles," p. 98.

‡ De Santis, "Historia di Napoli," p. 151.

The numerous communities of priests in Naples assembled, by order of Cardinal Filomarino. Jesuit, Theatine, and Franciscan, with crosses and lighted tapers in their hands, were followed by a number of youths bearing torches, and formed the first detachment of the mournful cavalcade. It was succeeded by the bier, on which, beside the mortal remains of the hero, were laid the bâton of a Marshal and an unsheathed sword. The pall of costly white damask was borne by the captains of the militia, who were followed by their several companies with arms reversed and standards lowered.*

A vast multitude of men, women, and children succeeded in the mournful train, and a low funeral chant, wailed forth by thousands of voices, rose with the solemn sounds of the Litany sung by the priests, upon the midnight air, which echoed the toll of bells and the beat of muffled drums. It was the requiem of a nation's grief.

The windows of the houses were illuminated in order that the procession might be fully seen.†

* Capecelatro, "Diario," p. 104. Tontoli, "Il Masaniello," p. 155.

† De Santis, "Historia di Napoli," p. 152.

Slowly the cavalcade wended its way through the several quarters of the city where the Sediles were held, and in passing the vicinity of the palace, the Spanish troops lowered their colours. Upon reaching the Cathedral of the Carmelites the remains of the Patriot of Naples were interred within the sacred building, where already reposed the dust of heroes whose memories are the most precious inheritance of Neapolitan history.

SUPPLEMENTARY CHAPTER.

I.

THE most sublime theories realized through the imperfect agency of humanity too often become so dwarfed and disfigured as to appear a mockery of the lofty conceptions out of which they sprang. The patriot, urged by a divine charity, which abandons the sterile regions of speculation for the operations of active benevolence, yearns to secure the choicest blessing of Freedom to an enslaved nationality. The highest sentiments which can animate the soul incite him to combat with ardour those influences which embitter the lot of his fellow-men by confining them in degrading servitude. He makes war against oppression, and is the originator of revolution.

And what, perhaps, is its fruit? Anarchy,

desolation, misery, bloodshed, and tears—all the dire elements of political discord—are its immediate consequences, instead of the progress, prosperity, and content suggested by the imagination of the reformer. Yet, if out of the passing chaos which necessarily attends convulsions of the national life—if at the cost of anguish, disaster, and even death—society, purified and elevated above the condition in which revolution found it, be ultimately benefited, the author of innovation has reason to rejoice.

What if, on the other hand, the best efforts of the patriot—the toils, the devotion of an existence to the cause of a people—be dedicated in vain? When treachery undermines, and diplomacy nullifies, the philanthropic work, when endurance is without reward, and martyrdom without victory,—then, indeed, a compassion, not without its piety, raises our admiration into reverence for the life that has been voluntarily sacrificed, but sacrificed in vain.

Thus it was in the insurrection under Masaniello. No valid reform and no abiding peace was secured to the State. A memorable protest had been made against despotism, but the Revolution had failed to achieve the triumph at which it aimed. After the lapse of more than two centuries—centuries during which the old persecutions from which the Neapolitans had suffered were certainly not materially lessened—the miseries of Naples, unameliorated under the sway of the execrable Bourbons, called for relief as piteously as they had done in the days when the Spanish viceroys ruled.

No national hero, no Masaniello, existed to answer the appeal, but a soul as lofty as his, a spirit as dauntless, a heart as disinterested, and an arm better inured to the service of the sword, were found to meet the summons when Garibaldi hastened to the deliverance of Naples.

As I have said, it was but a transitory calm, a hollow peace, that succeeded the fall of the Neapolitan hero. A chronic state of rebellion existed in the city. Not a day passed without the occurrence of tumults. These, increasing in virulence, constituted an insurrection more terrible, because more prolonged and aggravated, than the first.*

In the disorganized condition of the State, where the traditional ties of former authority had been suddenly snapped asunder, and were not yet replaced by other bonds of security and order, the slightest irritation of the populace gave rise

* Documenti, Archivio Storico Italiano, vol. ix.

to infuriated remonstrance. The old grievances still remained to excite an indignation that was exasperated into open and reckless defiance by the newly-discovered perfidy of the Spaniards, with respect to the Imperial Charter. A fatal clause introduced into the articles of the agreement between the Viceroy and People, that had constituted the basis of the Peace, rendered the concession of the Imperial rights, which the Neapolitans had hailed as the realization of their best hopes, utterly unavailing so far as their benefit was concerned. This clause contained a reservation of all such gabelles as were farmed out to private persons; and as we have seen how numerous were the farmers of tolls under the Viceroy, the abolition of taxes so fondly looked for was virtually an illusion.

This, however, was not the only complaint with the people. A strong reaction of feeling had succeeded the momentary torpor exhibited by the Neapolitans after the fall of Masaniello, and as the memory of their illustrious chief became sanctified in the minds of his followers, so much the more were they incensed at the impunity attending the crime of his assassination. Such was the fury they manifested against its perpetrators, that they were compelled to fly the kingdom, but were enriched ere their departure by a sum of money from the Viceroy as a reward for the deed.*

It is satisfactory to reflect that of all who took part in it, from the wretched hireling Catanco, by whose hand Masaniello was slain, to the base Genuino, by whom he was betrayed, not any one escaped the penalty due to his perfidy and guilt.

The fact of Genuino's elevation to office as President of the Chamber of Finance only accelerated his downfall. A trial in the very tribunal of which he was a member, concerning the incendiaries which had occurred during the Revolution of July, and in which he was proved by a document under his own signature to have been implicated, gave rise to an irrepressible clamour amongst the people. He escaped their fury, however, by a timely retreat, effected through the assistance of the Duke of Arcos, to the island of Sardinia, which, though virtually exile, his viceregal patron took care should be unattended with hardship. But this tranquil isolation was little suited to his turbulent intriguing temper, fostered by having lived in an atmosphere of strife. Fretting under compulsory inaction, he

* Baldacchini, "Storia Napoletana," p. 126.

still cherished, even in advanced age, dreams of self-aggrandizement, and sought to realize the aim of a low ambition by a wary participation in fresh tumults.

In this hope, he repaired to Spain, the scene of his former machinations aud misdemeanors, and thence to Port Mahon in Minorca, where this man—who had been, by turns, slave, fugitive, prisoner, the foe of a King and the friend of a Viceroy, who had been sentenced for high treason against the Spanish sovereign, and banished for having played false to the Revolution—closed his singular and mischievous career.* His name was vilified on all sides—by the nobility for having stimulated popular excesses—by the people for having betrayed the public cause. He left a memory such as few would desire to bequeath to posterity.

The spirit of rebellion that burned in the heart of Naples spread throughout the provinces, and burst forth simultaneously at all points of the kingdom. It raged in the feudal districts and in the royal cities. Neither Terra di Lavoro, Basilicata, Calabria, Apulia, nor the Abruzzi were free from the venom of sedition. In fact, so

* Baldacchini, "Storia Napoletana," p. 129.

powerful and extended had the Revolution become, that a fresh conquest of the kingdom or its entire abandonment by the crown of Spain appeared inevitable.

But it was in the Neapolitan capital that the storm expended itself most relentlessly. The market-place, the scene of so many tragedies, was, as before, the rallying point of the insurgents. Persevering with invincible determination in their course, they assailed some of the most important positions in the city. The custom-houses and the Convent of St Martino speedily fell into their hands, and they were proceeding in their victorious march when the artillery of the three fortress castles, St Elmo, Castel Nuovo, and Uovo, opened their murderous volleys on the people. War was now openly declared, and henceforward mercilessly waged. The work of destruction was carried on not only by the fire of the guns, but by hand to hand contests between the soldiery and the people, and during these death-grapples the streets of Naples were stained with the mingled blood of its citizens and its foes.*

The Revolutionists surpassed the Royalists in

* Documenti, Archivio Storico Italiano, vol. ix.

the rapidity with which they erected their defences. Within the city every street was intersected by trenches, and barricades were constructed in every available quarter. All the edifices in the hands of the people, which were situated at important points, were stoutly defended, and among these was the Vicarial or Castel Capuano, once considered as impregnable against assault. The revolutionary fortifications extended far beyond the limits of the city, and formed a strong line of defence from Poggio Reale to Posilippo. The entrenchments of the hostile factions marked out the city into two almost equal divisions, leaving the older or lower portion of the town towards the sea in the hands of the people.

The Royalists, meanwhile, commanded the upper part of Naples, the line of their defences commencing near San Martino, and passing along the ridge of the mountain to Porta Medina, and thence beyond Santa Chiara into the heart of the city onwards to the sea. These boundaries varied necessarily according to the advantages gained by the respective factions in the frequent skirmishes, involving bloodshed on either side; "but," says a noteworthy chronicler, "the loss on the part of the people, who held the most densely inhabited portion of the city, was not felt, owing to the vastness of the numbers in arms."*

No quarter was given to the vanquished. The Royalist troops were frequently worsted by the insurgents, and if so, whether Spaniard, German, or Walloon, were mercilessly sacrificed. Naples endured all the horrors of a state of siege. Supplies were cut off. The Royalists from their castles looked to the sea to obtain provisions, which were conveyed to them under the protection of Admiral Doria's fleet, while the insurgents contrived to keep open the roads to the south-east of Terra di Lavoro, in order to receive supplies from the town. Flour was doled out with the greatest parsimony, and even the districts hitherto most disposed to keep faith towards the Spanish crown were on the verge of revolt through want of bread.† It was now a rebellion in the full meaning of the word, for the movement had assumed an entirely novel character.‡ Hitherto royal authority, in name, at least, had been respected. Benedictions were showered on the sovereign, and no desire had

* Narrazione di Hermes Stampa.

†Ibid.

‡ Giannone, "Storia di Napoli," Libro xxxvii.

been exhibited for a change in the existing form of government. This deference to legitimate rule which redeemed the movement under Masaniello from the reproach of rebellion, was cast aside, and the kingly authority, as well as the local administration, was execrated and defied.

It was strange under these circumstances that the command of the popular forces should have been entrusted to Don Francesco Toraldo, an aristocrat who had been elevated to high honour and had received the most distinguished military title which could be conferred,* as a reward from the Spaniards for having gallantly defended Terragona against the French. He had therefore been created Field-Marshal and also the Prince of Massa. It is difficult to assign the motive that could have induced Toraldo to accept the post which the insurgents desired him to fill. It was certainly from no ambitious motive, since this brave and single-hearted soldier gave ample proof of his disinterestedness in refusing the rewards which the Neapolitans were eager to confer. Yet his actions, even when

* Documenti, Archivio Storico Italiano, vol. ix. p. 353.

holding office as leader of the people, do not tend to the conviction that he gave a cordial support to the movement, and before accepting command he desired a promise on oath that they would not wage war against the legitimate sway of the Spanish sovereign. Why, on the other hand, if he had no bias in favour of the popular cause, did he not again take arms in the service of the Royalists? It has been said, perhaps with truth, that no one ever resolves upon a fatal step without ample warning of the doom it will involve. Toraldo hesitated ere yielding to the pressing solicitations of the insurgents for him to be their commander. The tears and supplications of his lovely young wife were balanced against the vociferated demands of the multitude. Whether out of weakness, which could not withstand the popular entreaty, or owing to a conviction in favour of compliance, Don Toraldo assented to the wishes of the people.

Events soon proved the inexpediency of the measure, and he saw the evil of the false position in which it had placed him. The insurgents continued their course with unabated zeal. The fire of the Spaniards was returned from the batteries of the Revolutionists, who now desired to storm St Elmo.* The moment was critical, and the Viceroy felt it to be so. The troops were terrified at the idea of approaching famine. What if the French fleet, taking advantage of the crisis, should cut off the supplies by sea? The garrison at St Elmo murmured and declared their desire to abandon the fortress.

The Viceroy, meanwhile, persevered in the policy habitual to him. He temporized, deceived, and looked to others for the aid which should compensate for his own want of energy and influence. He relied upon Spain for succour, and he speculated hopefully upon the wavering policy pursued by Toraldo. Might not the popular cause again be lost, if not by the treachery, at least by the instability of those who called themselves its supporters? It was the turning point in the course of the insurrection. The insurgents were eager to attack Castel Nuovo as well as St Elmo. At the latter fortress they would in all probability have met with but a brief and feeble resistance from the half-hearted garrison who desired to abandon it. But the lukewarmness of Toraldo, their leader,

* Baldacchini, "Storia Napoletana," p. 132. Botta, "Storia d'Italia," vol. vi. p. 334.

deterred them by the suggestion of doubts, delays, insurmountable difficulties, and despair of conquest. Thus influenced, they desisted from the attack. Had their chief co-operated heartily with them, the speedy surrender of these fortresses would doubtless have placed the city in the power of the people, and the extermination of the Spaniards must have been the result.

The Viceroy had not counted in vain on the irresolution of Toraldo. The moment, therefore, appeared favourable for entering into fresh negotiations with the people, and Don Francesco encouraged the scheme by persuading them to come to terms. They were determined to put a high price upon their consent. They required the abolition of the noble Sediles, except two—the appointment of Neapolitans only to judicial and naval offices—the banishment of those who had suffered from the incendiaries of July as a further penalty, and the exile of several aristocratic families, including that of the Maddaloni. These demands were *openly* met by the Viceroy with a free consent except on one or two points, but were entertained *secretly* with that mental reservation by which the perjurer excuses to himself his broken vows. The Duke of Arcos, accordingly, did not hesitate to enter into a new treaty, which was publicly proclaimed on the 7th of September.*

The commotion at Naples, meanwhile, excited consternation at Madrid. The all-absorbing question arose as to what remedy should be applied to the intractable Neapolitan state? A policy of conciliation was resolved upon, a policy, however, which was to be backed by a demonstration of material force, so that, should negotiation prove fruitless, recourse might be had to arms. It was necessary, in order to facilitate an amicable adjustment, that a representative of Spanish interests should be selected whose courage might uphold the honour of his country, while his gentleness and courtesy should propitiate the nation which he sought to conciliate.

The lofty spirit and personal graces of the younger Don John of Austria, who combined a captivating personal appearance with kindly, affable manners, fitted him especially for the charge. He was therefore nominated commander of the fleet which appeared in the Gulf of Naples on the 1st of October, a fleet destined to serve the double purpose of defending the coast from the French and reducing the city to

* Baldacchini, "Storia Napoletana," p. 133.

obedience.* Don John refused to recognize the treaty that had already been entered into between the Viceroy and the people, until the latter had laid down their arms. This the unfortunate Toraldo sought to induce them to do. His efforts were useless, and their only result was to bring him into greater discredit with the populace, who already doubted his allegiance to their cause.

The first attempt at negotiation having signally failed, Don John, in an unguarded and luckless moment, allowed himself to be driven to extreme measures by the malice of the Viceroy. On the night previous to the memorable 5th of October the crews of the Spanish fleet landed secretly and joined the troops in Castel Nuovo and elsewhere. At a prearranged signal from the castle, the several fortresses simultaneously opened fire on the lower part of the town occupied by the insurgents. All was confusion and terror at this sudden alarm. No sooner was the roar of cannon heard than the citizens rushed to uplift the red standard on the tower adjacent to the market-place. The repeated volleys that swept the streets and shattered the buildings

* Giannone, "Storia civile di Napoli," Libro xxxvii.

could not drive them back, and the batteries they had erected speedily thundered in return against the strongholds of the foe. The struggle continued to be relentlessly carried on. For days the city was a prey to the worst horrors of civil war. The Royalists, under cover of their artillery, succeeded in taking the Pizzofalcone, but at other points they were valiantly repulsed by the people,* until the perpetual recurrence of massacres and assaults amid which Don John saw his best troops cut down, and his fleet severely injured, made him determine to withdraw his squadron to Baiæ.

Naples continued to be the scene of repeated tragedies. Don Toraldo, notwithstanding his strong desire for peace, was compelled, by the nature of his position, when called upon by the people, to second their measures by active service. Indeed, he dared not now retreat from the embarrassing situation into which he had been entrapped. He was called upon by the insurgents to lead an attack against Santa Chiara—a strong position of the Royalists—which hitherto had been found impregnable by the Revolutionists. The enterprise proved sig-

* Botta, "Storia d'Italia," vol. vi. p. 333.

nally disastrous in itself and in its consequences. The train of the mine which had been sprung under the tower having been improperly laid, burst only to scatter the neighbouring buildings far and near, and to crush numbers of the insurgents themselves under their ruins. The garrison of the place perceiving the disorder, sallied forth and forced back the assailants. A cry of "treason" was instantly raised, and the failure of the enterprise was attributed to the treachery of its leader. In the mad excitement of the moment, all sense of right or justice was lost, and an act of unparalleled cowardice and cruelty was committed, when Don Toraldo, roughly seized, was carried a prisoner to the market-place. Made captive without warning, he was sentenced without even a form of trial, and at once beheaded. A stone fish stall of the market served as the executioner's block in this atrocious deed of blood. With a malignity unworthy the basest of humanity, the assassins took the heart of the murdered man out of the still warm remains, and carried it on a dish to the convent, where the wife of Toraldo—the young and lovely Alvina—had taken refuge. They then commanded her to appear before them to receive the ghastly trophy of their crime. The sisters, with a pious charity, sought to shield the unhappy wife from such torture, but were told they would soon see their convent in flames if the request was not complied with. Donna Alvina, informed of the threatening danger, heroically appeared, and received the melancholy offering.*

* Narrazione di Hermes Stampa.

II.

In proportion as Don Francesco Toraldo, the patrician leader of revolution, lost favour with the people, another had contrived to gain their esteem. This was Gennaro Annese, a man without a single attribute of mind or character calculated to win regard.

According to a natural law of re-action where homage is heedlessly transferred in the impulse of the moment from one object to another, the allegiance of the people was given a second time, to one who presented, in every respect, a total contrast to Don Francesco Toraldo. The popular instinct henceforward repudiated all aristocratic associations, and in casting them off the insurgents imagined themselves safe, forgetting that danger might lurk in subjection to influences as destructive though of an entirely opposite nature.

Marc Antonio Brancaccio, a nobleman who had for many years fought in the service of the Venetian Republic, aspired to fill the post of command left vacant by the death of Toraldo. Brancaccio, notwithstanding his well-known hatred of the Spaniards, had little chance of success in the present temper of the people. The very fact that he was a noble was sufficient to ensure his defeat, and the appointment was awarded in preference to Gennaro Annese, who was created Captain-General of the revolutionary forces. This man, without a single attractive quality, whose exceeding ugliness was rendered still more repulsive by his want of cleanliness; vulgar in bearing, and coarse in manner; presented a marked contrast to the aristocratic type. His external appearance was the faithful index of a nature sordid, low, and base, insatiable in desire for gain, and unscrupulous as to the means of obtaining it.*

Annese had shown himself the uncompromising adversary of Toraldo, and Annese it was, who by encouraging the insurgents in the belief of their leader's treachery had incited them to the

* Giannone, "Storia civile di Napoli," Libro xxxvii.

sacrifice of Don Francesco. Stained with the blood of this brave and guiltless soldier, Annese succeeded to his command, and was admitted also to a share in the government of the kingdom, in conjunction with a council known as the Council of the People.* Entrusted by the Neapolitans with the very highest responsibility, he betrayed their cause by dictating the fatal policy of introducing a fresh foreign dominion into the State.

The disorganized condition of the kingdom caused it to be rife in political factions. The occupation of Naples by the Anjou princes had not existed for centuries without leaving a strong French bias in certain sections of the community. A yet stronger influence than this was the conviction in the minds of many, a conviction having its deep roots in the religion of a people intensely Catholic, in favour of papal rule. A majority again, comprising those engaged in trade, in the law courts, in public offices, professional men, artists and artisans, for whom peace was imperative in order to ensure progress in their several vocations, adhered to the rule of Spain, desiring only reform, not revolution. Another and in-

* Baldacchini, "Storia Napoletana," p. 145.

fluential, though smaller, class, supported the idea of a republic, to which the impulse of the age, as shown in the example of Holland, strongly tended. Moreover the transition from a principle we have discarded to another exactly opposite is easy. The multitude who now execrated the name of monarchy would soon learn to reverence that of a republic. A manifesto indeed had been issued by the Neapolitans previously to the Treaty of the 7th of September, in which they had set forth their grievances, and implored the aid, alternately, of pope, emperors, and kings. This sufficiently indicated the distracted state of opinion. Naples felt unable to contend alone against the despotism that threatened to overwhelm her.*

Then, as in every other political crisis of the kind, there were those who sought to trade upon this wretched condition of affairs, and were eager to turn the current of popular feeling in whatever direction best suited their interests. Impostors, whilst professing to be democrats, were leagued on the one hand with Spain, and on the other with France. Gennaro Annese was among the latter. Whilst these intriguers were endeavour-

* Botta, "Storia d'Italia," vol. vi. p. 336.

ing to carry out their schemes for the subjection of the kingdom afresh to a foreign yoke, Naples received the mock title of Republic.*

The Viceroy meantime continued dejected and helpless, having failed to obtain material assistance from Don John of Austria. His only hope now lay in forming an alliance with the feudal nobility, who, exiled, impoverished, and homeless, burned to avenge the spoliation and sufferings they had endured, and were ready to join any league of retribution against their plunderers. They did not hesitate, therefore, to meet the appeal of the Duke of Arcos, but with instantaneous obedience, armed at their own expense, hastened a powerful body to the field. The danger was imminent, and threatened the entire kingdom. The districts, severally under the sway of the Medicis, the Piccolomini, the Borghese, the Caetani, the Pignatelli, and the territories of Maddaloni, had more or less revolted.

The Duke of Nocera saw his palace burnt and his domestics slain in his presence. He himself was in peril of his life, and escaped with difficulty.

In some instances, as in the case of Nardo, which had rebelled against its ruler, the Count of

* Botta, "Storia d'Italia," vol. vi. p. 337.

Conversano, a fearful revenge was taken by the lords of the soil. The insurgents of Nardo had been on the first outbreak reduced to submission, and had received pardon. The Count, relying upon their apparently restored allegiance, had repaired to Conversano, where fresh tumults had arisen. No sooner had the ruler of Nardo departed, than his subjects again rose in revolt, but soon found reason to repent the outrage. This time no lenity was shown by Girolamo Acquaviva, Count of Conversano, who, a second Eccellino in tyranny, was called in derision the "Cyclops." His troops appeared before the walls of Nardo as the heralds of a direful retribution, for then ensued an indiscriminate slaughter, in which four canons of the cathedral, and many others, having no part in the Revolution, no less than the leaders of the people, were ruthlessly sacrificed."* An aged Baron was hanged by one foot, and so numerous were the deaths by hanging that a certain quarter was afterwards known as the "Gallows Street."

At the summons of the Viceroy the uprising of the Barons was universal, and fresh numbers continued daily to swell the army of defence.

* Capecelatro, "Diario," p. 159.

The family feuds, so frequent during the middle ages, and which had continued through centuries, were set aside. Baronial banners were unfurled, and mediæval arms taken up, far and near, to meet one common end. It was a second Barons' War.

The greater part of the troops commanded by these lords of the soil consisted of cavalry, and by these regiments it was that a panic was invariably created amongst the insurgents. Yet, upon the whole, the feudal forces presented a motley gathering. Horsemen and foot-soldiers mingled somewhat grotesquely with peasants fresh from the plough, household retainers, bravoes, and banditti, an assemblage strangely contrasted in arms and equipment; but if amidst its numbers, broken ranks and want of discipline might not unfrequently be detected, such drawbacks were compensated for by the untamed ardour of the men, and the unity of spirit animating the several leaders of the companies. The resources at the command of the Barons, notwithstanding sedition within their territories, may be inferred from the forces raised in individual cases. The Marquis del Vasto, whose ancestry had owned a glorious martial fame, brought one hundred and ninety horse and two hundred and twenty infantry into the field. But the number was slight compared with the amount raised by Don Diomed Carafa, the Duke of Maddaloni, whose name is so familiarly associated with the Revolution of 1647. Three hundred and fifty cavalry and three hundred and fifty-two foot-soldiers followed him in the war; a force far exceeding that supplied by the Piccolomini or Caraccioli.

The house of Carafa, the first of the feudal aristocracy of the time in wealth and power, had for this reason been assailed most persistently by the Revolutionists, and had suffered in proportion at their hands. Don Diomed did not forget the ignominious and tragic fate of Don Giuseppe, his brother. A price had been set upon his own head, his palace had been laid waste, his property annihilated, and he was under sentence of banishment. All this was the work of the plebeians, and for these unremitting outrages he longed to be avenged.

At an earlier period of the Revolution, when the nobility had been first assaulted by the populace, the Viceroy had made no effort to shield them from destruction. Indeed, had it served his purpose to do so, the Duke of Arcos would not have hesitated to inaugurate a hollow peace over the ruin of the entire aristocracy. Thus it had happened that Don Diomed, without hope of redress from the delegate of Spain, whose monarchs owed so much to his warlike predecessors, had, when outlawed by the people in the first instance, repaired to Florence and to Rome. Neither at the palace of the Medici, nor at that of his cousin, Cardinal Carafa, did the fugitive Don Diomed meet with a cordial reception. Pope Innocent wished to observe neutrality with regard to Spain, and he abstained, therefore, from interfering in the affairs of Naples. His secretary had written word to the Nuncio to avoid any negotiations with the people which might lead to unpleasant misunderstandings. Don Diomed remained but a few hours, consequently, in the palace of his cousin, and even for permitting this short visit the Cardinal was severely reproved by the Pontiff.

The Medicean ruler at Florence shared this policy of non-intervention, and actually refused to receive Carafa at all.

But it had become now the interest of the Viceroy to look to the nobility, or at least to require of them the aid he had failed to receive elsewhere. It suited them to seek retaliation for their own wrongs, and without further deliberation they resolved upon a campaign, the immediate object of which was to clear the environs of Naples from the numerous bands of insurgents who occupied the passes, and thus confine the insurrection to a narrower arena within the capital.

The baronial chiefs and their followers assembled at Capua, and in the picturesque plain at the foot of the mighty Vesuvius, which terminates one of the most enchanting prospects in the universe, the war between the patricians and plebeians was inaugurated.

The difficulties attending the campaign were not inconsiderable for the Royalists. They were continually surprised and often defeated by the enemy, who were strongly entrenched at available points amidst the heights adjacent to Naples. In the hiding-places afforded by the thick wood of these natural defences, the insurgents were almost impregnable.* Their assailants knew not at what point to aim, for the rapidity of their movements at the first signal of attack usually rendered the assault entirely without result, as they retreated in safety under cover of the shelter afforded them by nature. If the Royalists succeeded in taking one situation, fresh numbers of the foe, pouring

* Narrazione di Hermes Stampa.

out of the nooks in these mountain forests, compelled them to abandon it. This irregular warfare, tedious in its operation, was destructive in its effects. The utmost energy in action on the part of the Barons would prove fruitless when baffled by some sudden and unaccountable change of tactics by their adversaries. Disorder followed on surprise, and failure was the consequence. The insurgents, holding the position of besieged, had the advantage in situation so long as the original positions were maintained. The commencement of the campaign was, therefore, but little encouraging to the Barons.

Don Vincenzio Tuttavilla, commissioned by the Viceroy, had hastened with a small body of troops, valuable not on account of numbers, but from the fact of their having been inured to service, to hold a council of war at Capua. The plan of operation decided upon was to chase the insurgents from the outskirts of Naples. Tuttavilla proceeded, accordingly, to endeavour to clear the line of communication between Pozzuoli and the capital. But here the insurgents, who had erected strong defences, offered a valiant and successful resistance, and here the illustrious Don Vincenzio Tuttavilla, who had been installed by the Viceroy in high office as commander-in-chief of the united army, and whom, after some demur, the assembly of ducal captains had consented to obey, was driven to an ignominious retreat.

The next encounter under the same leader brought no more glory to the aristocratic arms. In an enterprise against the village of Marano, between Pozzuoli and Aversa, Tuttavilla was surprised by a sortie of the enemy. Hopeless confusion spread through the ranks of his followers, who, in their dismay, were cut down on every side. The remainder of the fugitive band returned with news of the disaster to Aversa.

Commanders bearing names of no less renown than Tuttavilla were actively employed in other directions. Don Alfonso Piccolomini, son of the Count of Celano, repaired at the head of his troops from Castellamare, his ancestral territory, to Torre dell Annunziata, a place important to defend, because it contained the corn-mills upon which the town depended for supplies of flour. Piccolomini succeeded at first in repulsing the attack upon the tower in which he was entrenched, and drove back the assailants with loss. But as fresh numbers hastened to the assault, he felt it to be impossible to hold out much longer. His only hope in this dilemma was to receive succour from the body of troops which he knew were collected under Don Carlo Capecelatro in the village of St Anastasia. The difficulty was how to apprize Capecelatro of the peril in which he stood. At length he succeeded in finding a trustworthy messenger, who bore the tidings to Don Francesco. He at once held council with several nobles as to the course to be pursued in order to relieve Piccolomini.

The majority decided that the united forces at their command were insufficient to hazard an open march in the face of a multitude of armed peasants, and wanted to relinquish the enterprise altogether. Capecelatro bravely declared his determination to proceed at all risks to the rescue of Piccolomini. The remainder of the party, shamed by his superior courage, then resolved to go with him. Midway in their route they were met by Piccolomini and his few followers, who, instead of waiting for succour, had succeeded in making a sortie from their quarters. The entire gathering then returned together to Torre dell Annunziata. There they were gladdened by the news that the Duke of Maddaloni intended to bring a reinforcement of three hundred men on the morrow if they could maintain their position until then. Everything promised well for the defence of Torre dell Annunziata.

Scarcely had evening closed, however, ere the steeples of the various churches rang an alarm throughout the country. A fresh agitation stirred the Revolutionists, who had marched in several directions, and had made captive many of the nobles and of the opulent citizens. In the midst of these disasters elsewhere, intelligence reached the cavaliers at Torre dell Annunziata, that the Duke Don Diomed had been in consequence delayed by insurmountable obstacles on the road. The siege of the tower, meanwhile, was continued with unrelenting vigour. Panic seized the garrison, and, taking advantage of a pause in the assault, they sallied forth under cover of the darkness, and mounting their horses, fled in haste to Nola, a town whither sedition had not yet spread. During the journey the most disheartening news met them on every side, till, in despair, they wished to retire to Castellamare. But the approaches to it were strictly guarded. The united forces then determined to separate, in order the better to avoid observation and facilitate escape. Piccolomini and Capecelatro rode on till they reached a spot opposite the mouth of the Sarno, and passing the stream undetected, reached Castellamare in safety. The others, who pursued their course through the interior of the country, encountered greater difficulties in their flight.

A repetition of such reverses would speedily have prostrated the energies of the Royalists. But Fortune, hitherto so adverse, brought them triumph with her changes. Their operations were more successfully conducted in the north. Aversa, between Naples and the fief of Maddaloni, yielded to the renowned Prince of Montesarchio. The conqueror destroyed the mills and aqueducts, to the dismay of the inhabitants of Naples. Owing to the scarcity of water in the city, the loss of the aqueducts was severely felt. Indeed, so furious were the people, that they caused the sisters of the offender, nuns in the Convent of Saint Gaudioso, to be seized by way of retaliation, and openly threatened their honour and their life in case the prince did not make reparation. The sisters, in this terrible emergency, wrote an urgent appeal to their brother, who, with cruel firmness, persisted in not conceding to the wishes of the people, but he declared that if they dared to carry out their insulting threats, he would never rest till he had reduced Naples to ashes.*

Victory at the same time was on the side of the Royalists elsewhere, for at Aversa, where the

* Narrazione di Hermes Stampa.

insurgents under Lautrec had halted, the revolutionary ranks were broken up with terrible slaughter by the Imperialists, while their expeditions in the south-east were effectively carried on. This series of conquests on the part of the Royalists entirely altered the position of the combatants.

The miseries of war now pressed with the utmost severity upon the insurgents, for the feudal lords and their lawless followers took good care that desolation and cruelty should mark their triumphant course. Farms and homesteads were scattered to the winds, fields made waste, and cattle destroyed. Naples was reduced to the direst need. Communication with the provinces was next to impossible, for the roads, now commanded by the different Royalist leaders, were jealously guarded. Neither by land nor water could the people look for supplies. Repeated sallies from the town, though bravely performed, assisted them but little. Famine and utter ruin constituted the sole prospect for the future. Driven to desperation, they resolved to carry by force the passes to Salerno. In order to do this, it was necessary to gain the bridge over the Sarno at Scafati, which was in possession of the Spaniards. A fortified tower formed the *tête de pont* of the position. Gennaro

Annese resolved to lead an attack against this tower. It was but slenderly garrisoned, and deficient in provisions and ammunition. The only chance of succour for the besieged was from Castellamare. The assailants were careful, therefore, to blockade the approaches to that place, whilst under the shelter of the earth-works they had thrown up they continued to fire against the tower. The Spaniards showed the utmost energy in the defence, but the courage which could resist the assault from without could not hope to stand against hunger. The assailants, aware of this, were determined to conquer the besieged by starvation if they could not by other means. To such straits were the Spaniards reduced, they had to tear up the linen they wore in order to make wadding for their guns.

The small Royalist force at Castellamare, under Pietro Carafa, was not sufficient alone to succour the Spaniards in their extremity. Don Pietro, therefore, called in the aid of Tuttavilla, who lost no time in obeying the summons. This measure was the salvation of the besieged. A detachment of the Royalists advanced at once from Somma, and meeting with a party of insurgents, put them to instant flight. Tuttavilla, then arriving with the remainder of his forces, led on the attack against those who were storming the tower. The infantry, who were the first to assail, succeeded in scattering the enemy. The cavalry followed up the advantage, while the Spaniards poured a sharp fire from the walls upon those who tried to escape by the bridge, where the passage was contested in a ferocious hand-to-hand struggle. The insurgents, completely routed, were pursued for miles by the conquering cavalry of their opponents. Above two hundred and fifty of the vanquished were killed, and as many were made prisoners. The track of their flight was strewn with the dead and dying. In the last agony they showed devotion to their cause. One of those mortally injured wrote with the life-blood flowing from his wound the letter P for *Popolo,* on the sand. Only those of the insurgents who reached the mountains, and could thus defy the terrors of the cavalry, escaped.

No quarter was given in general by the Royalist troops. On the other hand the aristocratic leaders, mixed up in this irregular warfare, met with the strangest adventures, were reduced to dire extremities, and often narrowly escaped with their lives. This was the case with Don Francesco Capecelatro, in his flight from Somma, where the insurgents had threatened to kill him. Capecelatro, disguised in a shabby suit of the costume worn by the knights of St Jago, set out on horseback, and pursued his fugitive course along the least frequented thoroughfares, and made his way unmolested to Fratta. Here everything was in commotion, owing to a tumult amongst the peasantry. Suspicion was aroused by Don Capecelatro's arrival, and the people insisted on his entering their trenches, under pretence that he would thus be more sheltered in case of attack. Immediate compliance seemed most expedient when resistance was impossible. In the trenches Capecelatro met another fugitive, who, like himself, had thrown off the decorations of his military rank, and was attired as a common soldier. This man warned Capecelatro, whom he recognized in spite of his disguise, to observe the greatest caution, since in case of discovery they would be inevitably assassinated. Capecelatro succeeded, however, after some trouble and contrivance, in taking his departure. His object now was to reach a Franciscan Convent adjacent. Whilst hastening over the fields in a cross direction to avoid a close encounter with a party of Revolutionists, whom he perceived in the distance, he fell into a ditch, and lost the cloak which formed an essential part of his disguise. On his approach to the convent, he found fresh difficulties to surmount. It was necessary to climb the convent wall, and, owing to its height, the leap on the other side would have been a perilous one in any case. But what was Capecelatro's dismay to perceive a deep abyss below, threatening to make the plunge a fatal one. Yet there was danger in delay, and Don Francesco, with his habitual intrepidity, hesitated not a moment, and cleared the wall in safety. The fugitive was heartily welcomed by the inmates of the convent, with whom, however, he made only a short stay, but before setting out again was advised by the prior to take off his boots, which he had retained by an oversight, and which would at once have betrayed the fact that he was an aristocrat and a Royalist. A priest, accordingly, presented him with a pair of very old shoes, "so large," says the chronicler of this strange adventure, "that two of my feet would have gone with ease into one of them." With the difficulties of pedestrianism thus increased, Capecelatro had to pursue his journey on foot, since it was impossible to find a horse, through by-ways to Aversa, where he joined the Royalist troops, who were preparing for action.

In the midst of continued tumults, attempts were still made to negotiate. Defeat and victory had as yet been so closely balanced as to render the campaign, notwithstanding recent triumphs on the part of the Barons, an inconclusive one. It was not easy to maintain the blockade of a city so extensive and so populous as that of Naples, nor to keep in check the peasantry throughout so large an arena as that under revolt. Subdued at one point, they invariably broke out afresh at another, and it seemed impossible to extirpate an insurrection, at least by force of arms, at once so deeply-rooted and so widely spread. The Barons, eager for peace, would gladly have acceded to whatever terms were proposed, provided they were not actually dishonourable. They appealed to Don John of Austria to negotiate for them, but Don John failed as signally as at first in this second attempt to come to an agreement with the people.

The Viceroy meantime followed his usual course of duplicity. Without faith himself, he inspired no confidence in others. Whilst he assured the Duke of Maddaloni of his gratitude for his energetic service, and praised him as he had praised Masaniello, calling him the deliverer of his country in public, in his private correspondence with the Pope he declared that it was the aristocracy who were the stumbling-block in the way of coming to a good understanding with the people.

The perplexity attending this distracted condition of affairs was solved by an event which no longer left the settlement of matters in the hands of the local government. This was the entry of Henri de Guise, Duke of Lorraine, who had for some time cherished the project he now carried out. Many reasons had urged him to the enterprise. The remembrance of the submission of Naples throughout centuries to the Anjou sovereigns; his knowledge of the existing faction in his favour; the fact that the very name of Guise, associated as it was with the support of Catholicism, would be hailed with gladness by the Neapolitans—all these considerations led Lorraine to conclude that his entry would not be discountenanced by them. Naples, which had ever been the apple of discord between the Houses of Arragon and Anjou, he regarded indeed belonging as by right to his race, and he entertained the greatest confidence that he would not be scouted either by nobility or people. Henri de Guise, descendant of Le Balafré, was not without that ambition which was the leading attribute of his family. Young, valiant, and endowed with brilliant qualities of mind and person, he could scarcely fail to succeed, he thought, in the enterprise on which his heart was fixed.

On the 16th of November, in the year 1647, the Duke of Lorraine embarked, accompanied by a limited suite, at Fiumicino. The voyage was short, but perilous, for the Duke had to watch carefully against detection by the Spanish fleet. He, however, landed in safety, and was received amidst the din of artillery and the joyful shouts of an enthusiastic assembly.* A majority of the Neapolitans rejoiced at any change which should ensure their release from Spanish bondage, and were naturally inclined to favour a deliverer of noble demeanour, courteous manners, and who moreover addressed them in their own musical language.

Henri de Guise, after immediately returning thanks in the Cathedral for his prosperous journey, sought Gennaro Annese, who was lodged in the tower of the Carmine. A graphic description is given by the Duke of his sojourn with the armourer,† and the amusing contrast thus

* Giannone, "Storia civile di Napoli," Libro xxxvii.

† Memoires du Duc de Guise.

suggested between the aristocrat Guise, handsome, luxurions, and refined, and Gennaro Annese, coarse, hideous, and repulsive, is in itself sufficiently striking to form an interesting picture. But the amicable relation existing between two men so entirely opposed by nature and by fortune was not likely, nor was it destined, to endure.

The Duke of Guise was presented with a consecrated sword, and was formally installed as chief of the Neapolitan Republic. Notwithstanding the fact that these honours were accorded him, the situation of Henry of Lorraine was a hazardous and an unenviable one. The enthusiasm of the people was scarcely to be relied upon. The small number of the Duke's suite and his comparative poverty, soon exposed him to the ridicule of the facetious among the crowd, who exclaimed *"é arrivato il Duca Chisa"* * (Chi sa), thus by a perversion of his title throwing doubts upon his identity and the validity of his claims. In order to counterbalance the effect of these mocking comments, the Duke sought to uphold his popularity by improving the condition of the city. He formed a regiment at his own expense of the prisoners of war, who

* Baldacchini, "Storia Napoletana," p. 148.

had been hitherto most cruelly murdered, and did his utmost to suppress disorders.* Continued tumult, nevertheless, marked the close of the memorable year 1647. Six months of revolution had followed upon centuries of tyranny, and Naples, desolated and distracted, was reaping the bitter fruits of both. The desire for peace had augmented, but the Royalists themselves, who were especially anxious for a pacification, could not but acknowledge that the presence of the Duke of Arcos constituted an insurmountable obstacle to the conciliation of the Revolutionists. Such, indeed, was the conviction at Madrid. The Duke of Arcos consequently was recalled, aud after two years of authority, which he had exercised with mischievous influence, he surrendered the Viceregal office, and departed, amidst the execrations of the people, on the 26th of January, 1648.

In spite of the daring and triumphant entry of Guise into Naples, he failed to render his position secure by a judicious improvement of the advantages he had gained. Reckless in expression, self-indulgent, and somewhat frivolous, he contrived to make bitter enemies, whose

* Giannone, "Storia civile di Napoli," Libro xxxvii.

machinations he had not the acumen to fathom, nor the stedfastness persistently to oppose. Gennaro Annese, once his intimate associate, had soon become his implacable foe,* and, jealous of the superior position occupied by Guise, resolved, if possible, to undermine his power. But the Duke was more than all the victim of his own injudicious conduct, and thus it happened that the most auspicious occasion which had ever offered itself to France for the subjugation of the Spanish dominion in Italy, was offered in vain. Exactly at the moment when the critical state of affairs in Naples called most particularly for the presence of Guise, he left the city in order to engage in an enterprise as misjudged as it was mistimed. This was the conquest of the little island of Nisida,† whence he hoped to command Pozzuoli. Whilst the artillery of Guise was firing on the fort of the island, and the Duke himself was waiting in the camp for news of its expected surrender, momentous events were taking place within Naples. A well-combined movement on the part of the Royalist commanders brought the entire strength of their forces to

* Botta, "Storia d'Italia," p. 347.

† Giannone, "Storia civile di Napoli," Libro xxxvii.

bear upon the capital. The force of the insurrection had already given way, and but comparatively little resistance was offered to the Spaniards, who, speedily asserting their supremacy, marched in triumph to the market-place, where the Revolution had its rise, and where it was now virtually extinguished.* The artistic genius of the time has left a representation of the stirring scene, where amidst the crowd of mounted nobles with their dancing plumes and magnificent equipments, is seen the figure of the young Don John of Austria, receiving the keys of the city from the dignitaries of the kingdom. The bronzed faces of the soldiery appear under lines of flashing steel in all directions, but conspicuous amidst the entire multitude is Gennaro Annese, who, sullen and relentless, laments the resignation of authority by the populace.

Upon receiving intelligence of the re-establishment of the Spaniards in Naples, the Duke of Guise made a feeble attempt to resist their recovered sway. But his very first effort to resume the war was fatally disastrous. Surprised by the cavalry of the enemy, his few followers were speedily scattered, and the Duke,

* Botta, "Storia d'Italia," p. 351.

after a valiant resistance with his sword, was compelled to surrender. He was sentenced to imprisonment in the fortress of Gaeta, and not until the wars of the Fronde did Henry of Lorraine recover his freedom.

Gennaro Annese, who was suspected of conspiring a second time in favour of the French, was imprisoned, and at length executed, a fate well deserved by the assassin of Don Francesco Toraldo.

III.

If the conquest of Naples by Spain was achieved at the sore cost of the Neapolitans, it was a victory for which Spain herself also paid dearly. The possession of this fairest portion of the Italian territory proved, indeed, a source of perpetual disquietude to the sovereigns of the sister peninsula, whose armaments and administrations were often powerless to suppress the chronic disaffection and anarchy that existed within the limits of the Neapolitan dominions. The Spanish monarchs had to contend against a double evil, for added to the danger of defiance to their rule from rebellion in the State was the constant menace of another power, diligently on the watch to usurp the authority of Spain in Naples. Fleets intended for the intimidation of the enemy without, found, on arriving at their destination, employment for their fire in quelling the foe within; and thus it had happened that the squadron under Don John of Austria, destined to guard the Neapolitan shores from French aggression, had found it imperative to turn its volleys on the Neapolitan people.

The busy conflict of faction at Naples, with its schemes and counter-schemes, intrigues and hostilities, rendered diplomacy a difficult task, and not the best efforts of those selected by the court of Madrid as its representatives could give satisfaction to perplexed, uneasy monarchs, who imagined they found fresh adversaries in the very men to whose faith and integrity their interests were committed.

Hence it was that the enterprise under Don John of Austria, signally successful as it had been, was not brought to a close without giving umbrage to Spain. To the prompt and vigorous measures of the youthful commander it was that the suppression of the Revolution was mainly attributable, yet scarcely was his triumph complete, the insurrection quelled, and the keys of the city in his grasp, than jealousy and mistrust were engendered where only gratitude was due. The strictest deference to royal prerogative had been observed by Don John, who, notwithstanding his fidelity to the cause of Spain, was dear to the Neapolitans; but the high position won by his courage and wisdom was considered too full of allurement to young ambition to be longer filled with safety by its occupant. It was necessary that an influence which might become dangerous should at once be superseded by the appointment of a successor to the viceregal office, which had been left vacant since the departure of the Duke of Arcos. Don Inigo de Guevara, Count of Onate, was accordingly elected as Viceroy, and commissioned to proceed with all despatch to Naples.

The Count of Onate, like Don Pietro di Toledo of cruel memory, was a Viceroy of thoroughly Spanish stamp. Crafty, though austere and inflexible, he could simulate characteristics precisely opposite to those of his nature, in order to carry out measures which, once resolved upon, were not easily abandoned. He was devoted to the interests of Spain, which he was called upon to promote at a critical hour, in which there existed in more than one direction sufficient cause to arouse his habitual suspicion. The watchfulness of Onate was exercised especially with regard to the movements of France,* and long ere it had devolved upon him to assume the viceregal office, he had been actively engaged in thwarting French influence in Naples. Opposition is often most effectual when acting under a semblance of support, and treachery was proverbially congenial to Spanish Viceroys. Onate had from the first been acquainted with the schemes of the Duke of Guise, whom he hated, whose downfall he was determined upon, and whose entry into Naples he had looked forward to as the surest means of his destruction. The conduct of Onate with respect to the Duke of Guise fully reveals the character of the new Viceroy. He resolved to render the unstable Henry of Lorraine the victim of his own ambition, and favoured the enterprise he had in view up to the moment of its accomplishment, and the triumphal entry of Guise into Naples. But the real aim of the Count of Onate was not yet achieved, and continued machinations were essential to its accomplishment. A moment of exaltation, such as that in the career of Henry of Lorraine when he became the temporary ruler of Naples, is not propitious to the exercise of a wise judg-

* Baldacchini, "Storia Napoletana," p. 144.

ment, and the Count of Onate perceived that in establishing an influence over the mind of Lorraine, lay his best chance of success. He therefore entrusted a secret mission to Agostino Mollo, a ready and unscrupulous agent, who under a show of devoted adherence to the French cause, succeeded in gaining the confidence of Guise, and constituted himself his counsellor. The policy he dictated at the instigation of the Count of Onate, even to the last fatal step made by Guise in his ill-timed attack on Nisida, was destined to precipitate the downfall of Henry of Lorraine.*

His defeat was the signal for the reconquest of the capital by the Spanish arms, that delivered the city into the custody of Don John of Austria, upon which ensued the appointment of Don Inigo de Guevara to the viceregal office. He found Naples in utter anarchy, but to restore "order" was the chosen task of representatives of royal authority, such as Pietro di Toledo and Inigo de Guevara, who proceeded with the utmost energy to carry out his policy of repression. His first care was to reinforce the garrisons, improve the fortifications, despatch

* Baldacchini, "Storia Napoletana," p. 153.

armed bands against the few scattered remnants of the revolutionary forces which still occupied the Abruzzi, and to engage in vigorous action against the French, whom, in a joint compaign with Don John of Austria, he finally expelled from Elba and Piombino. Nor was he less diligent in labours of a pacific kind: restoring public works which the horrors of the insurrection had destroyed or defaced, and encouraging the pursuit of those tranquil studies which the tumult of revolutionary passion had retarded. Not only did he reinstate the professors of art and science in the enjoyment of their just emoluments and dignities, but even assisted personally in the intellectual exercises which engaged the professors of philosophy and their disciples.*

But salutary measures such as these were not considered by the Viceroy calculated alone to restore tranquillity to the State. The Neapolitans soon found that the promises of pardon for past offences that the Viceroy, upon his arrival, had pledged as lavishly as he had scattered small coins amongst the multitude, were not to be relied upon. Naples was everywhere pervaded by troops, and fast bound under the

* Botta, "Storia d'Italia," p. 356.

pressure of a military despotism. Confiscations, imprisonments, and executions on the most shallow charges, followed each other in such rapid succession as to recall the holocausts rendered to so-called justice under Don Pietro di Toledo. The rigour with which the new Viceroy governed the people was surpassed by the severity he exhibited towards the nobles, whose services and successes in the late war, it was thought, would increase their pride and pretensions, and were therefore remembered only to their disadvantage. The nobles, on the other hand, reflecting upon what they had lost themselves, no less than what they had acquired for another, looked for a double reward at the hands of royalty, and demanded entire provinces as adequate compensation. Malice is ingenious in discovering pretexts upon which to act. The new Viceroy dreaded, above all, the existence of conspiracies, and woe to those who were suspected of taking part in them. A rumour spread that a plot was formed with the object of placing Don John of Austria on the throne of Naples. In December of the year 1648, Andrea d'Avalos, the same prince of Montesarchio who had played so prominent a part as mediator during the Revolution of the preceding year, was seized in the king's name as a prisoner when on the point of setting out on a journey to Messina. Conveyed to the Castle dell' Uovo, he was there kept under strict guard. At the same time his brother, the Prince of Troya, was forbidden under a severe penalty to leave the city. He, however, contrived to escape, seeking refuge, first at Arienzo, a castle that belonged to the Duke of Maddaloni, whence he repaired to Benevento.

Soon after, the Prince of Roccella, Gregorio Carafa, who had so narrowly escaped with his life during the insurrection, was arrested. Montesarchio meanwhile languished in the dungeons of dell' Uovo. Not his nearest relatives were permitted to approach him, and such was the anguish of his mother, that it is said to have caused her death. In all these cases of arrest a rigid system of inquiry was carried on. The members of the household belonging to the several nobles accused, were kept in custody, and frequently put to the torture.

The consternation produced by these proceedings was immense. It seemed a return of the horrors under Toledo, whose policy was so closely followed by the new Viceroy, that the people every day dreaded another attempt to revive the Inquisition. They were often at a loss to discover the meaning of these arbitrary measures. In some instances, as in the case of the Prince of Montesarchio, so far from cause of punishment existing, there appeared every reason for a grateful recognition of past services, since he and the Duke of Maddaloni had distinguished themselves above all others as the valorous defenders of the Spanish cause. Vague rumours, indeed, suggested that the whole was the result of a discovery which had been made to the effect that the object of Montesarchio's journey to Messina was to promote the conspiracy in favour of Don John of Austria. But the Viceroy thought it expedient to proclaim another motive for the further measures he proposed to adopt. Accordingly, wholesale charges were brought against the feudal aristocracy, who were accused of having encouraged disturbances by sheltering banditti. Agostino Mollo, the agent of Onate and the confidant of Guise, was nominated by the Viceroy judge of the several districts whose owners were suspected, whilst the Barons themselves were summoned to the Neapolitan capital to answer for the conduct imputed to them. The lords of Avellino and Forino, the Piccolomini and the Maddaloni, with the Caraccioli, were desired to appear and be tried for their offences. The Caraccioli, with characteristic courage, refused to obey the mandate, neither would the Duke of Maddaloni appear, who felt that refusal in his case was especially justifiable. The family of Carafa had suffered far more than others in consequence of the Revolution. Don Diomed, moreover, had taken a prominent part in the services lately rendered to the Spanish sovereign. Hitherto, he had been sustained in his misfortunes by the hope of a final triumph, and had looked forward ardently to the day when he should enter Naples free to avenge the injuries suffered by himself and his race. The proud spirit of Don Diomed could ill brook the malice which would thus condemn him to further penalty. He had looked for reward, and found injustice. He would not yield to the tyrannical demand of the Viceroy, who accordingly determined on more decisive measures, and despatched an armed force to discover where the Duke was sheltered, and in the event of finding out the spot, were commissioned to storm the place. The approach of so formidable an armament induced the Duke to fly from the Castle of Arienzo, where he had taken up his abode, and where the plunder of arms and powder, after his departure, enriched the resources of his pursuers.

A rumour spread that Don Diomed had resolved to abandon altogether a country where his peace was perpetually outraged, and in which his most distinguished achievements were unrecognized. The Viceroy, in order to put an obstacle in the way of his flight, prevailed upon the Duchess, Don Diomed's wife, to visit Naples, where she was of course detained. The Duchess, meanwhile, was indefatigable in her endeavours to effect a reconciliation between her husband and the Viceroy, and succeeded at length in obtaining the pardon of the accused for the offences charged against him.

Once more Don Diomed entered the city from which he had been exiled for years. After a public thanksgiving for his felicitous return, he repaired to the royal palace to express his gratitude to the Viceroy. A throng of spectators assembled to catch a glimpse of the well-remembered "Duke of Maddaloni," but it was no longer the turbulent multitude which, with ferocious clamour, had dogged his steps in the time of the Revolution.

After so many strange alternations of fortune, it was now the fate of Don Diomed to enjoy repose for a season. This tranquil interval he employed in erecting a palace, which, for space and costliness of decoration, vied with the noblest ducal edifices of the 17th century. Here all the splendour of the lineage of Maddaloni was lavishly displayed, and here, surrounded by the fantastic luxury of the time, the Duke dwelt at ease, holding sumptuous revels, at which the Viceroy himself was one of the numerous guests, who, after a magnificent entertainment, received presents worthy of a royal fête.

The Duke of Maddaloni continued to enjoy a prosperous career until the close of the government of the Count of Onate, in the year 1653. At the expiration of five years the Duke was again involved in vexations, resulting partly from the violence of his own imperious temper, and partly from the agitations of the tumultuous period in which he lived. The members of the different sediles were often, as it has been shown, at variance, and in addition to these petty conflicts amongst themselves, disagreements frequently sprung up between the Piazze and the ecclesiastical courts. On the occasion of the festival of St Januarius, an altercation had arisen between the members of the Sedile of Capua and the Cardinal Filomarino with respect to the right of exercising certain privileges claimed by the former. In this contest Don Diomed acted an enthusiastic part, for the smallest matter was sufficient to revive the animosity which had ever existed between the Duke of Maddaloni and the Cardinal. The cavaliers of the Sedile of Capua wished to placard a protest against the restriction of the rights they claimed, but the paper had been torn from the hands of the notary by Filomarino. The Duke of Maddaloni, in revenge, snatched the document again out of the hands of the Cardinal, at the same time levelling at him a torrent of vituperation. But this scandalous scene cost the Duke dearly. The short-lived tranquillity of his recent career did not survive these events. He found himself once more the object of a series of aggressions, conspiracies, and penalties, which ended in sudden arrest and close confinement. Denied even the right of a trial, the Duke remained imprisoned in a Spanish fortress, where he languished in wretchedness until the year 1660, when death closed his strangely fitful existence. The character of Diomed, Duke of Maddaloni, presents a fair type of the feudal aristocracy of the day. Lawless and self-indulgent to the last degree, the nobles were, nevertheless, for the most part devoted to the monarchy of Spain, which they served with courage always, and occasionally with a self-sacrifice truly heroic.

The study of Neapolitan history, as developed under the Viceroys of Spain, helps to elucidate the causes of her subsequent misery and degradation. We cannot, indeed, understand the nature of the ills from which she has suffered in modern times without investigation of their origin, which we find in the evils inflicted upon her by foreign despotism at an earlier date, for, if the tyranny of the Bourbons merits execration, the bitterness of their rule was equalled, if not surpassed, under the dominion of Spain.

THE END.

CPSIA information can be obtained
at www.ICGtesting.com
Printed in the USA
LVHW111958050422
715401LV00006B/269

9 783752 589023